FATAL JUDGMENT

ANDY HAYES MYSTERIES

by Andrew Welsh-Huggins

FATAL
JUDGMENT

AN ANDY HAYES MYSTERY

ANDREW WELSH-HUGGINS

SWALLOW PRESS
OHIO UNIVERSITY PRESS
ATHENS

Swallow Press
An imprint of Ohio University Press, Athens, Ohio 45701
ohioswallow.com

Printed in the United States of America
Swallow Press / Ohio University Press books are printed on acid-free paper ⊗ ™

28 27 26 25 24 23 22 21 20 19   5 4 3 2 1

Library of Congress Cataloging-in-Publication Data
Names: Welsh-Huggins, Andrew, author.
Title: Fatal judgment : an Andy Hayes mystery / Andrew Welsh-Huggins.
Description: Athens, Ohio : Swallow Press, 2019. | Series: Andy Hayes
   mysteries
Identifiers: LCCN 2018056388 | ISBN 9780804012119 (hardcover) | ISBN
   9780804041027 (pdf)
Subjects: LCSH: Private investigators--Fiction. | Missing
   persons--Investigation--Fiction. | BISAC: FICTION / Mystery & Detective /
   General. | GSAFD: Mystery fiction.
Classification: LCC PS3623.E4824 F38 2019 | DDC 813/.6--dc23
LC record available at https://lccn.loc.gov/2018056388

For the real Pete Henderson,

who always guessed the

Encyclopedia Brown clues first.

"I'm sorry, Dave. I'm afraid I can't do that."

—HAL 9000, from *2001: A Space Odyssey*

"Make Google Do It."

—Television ad for the Google Assistant

1

A BIRD WHOSE SONG I didn't recognize was singing high in the tree beside me when the car pulled up to the curb. Black Lexus sedan, newer model, semi-tinted windows. I stepped forward, hearing the click of the passenger door unlocking. I opened the door, glanced at the driver, and slid inside.

"Sure you don't want to come in?"

"I'm sure," Laura Porter said, staring straight ahead.

I shut the door. "It's good to see you."

She nodded but didn't respond. It was early evening on a Monday in mid-August, shadows stretching across the street toward my house as dusk descended. I heard laughter down the way at Schiller Park as dog walkers gathered, and the sound of a car engine cutting off as someone scored a lucky parking space behind us. Inside, Laura's Lexus smelled of coffee, Armor All, and above all her perfume.

"So," I said.

Seconds that might have been centuries passed in silence as she studied her windshield. Her hands remained on the steering wheel, knuckles as white as if she were navigating a hairpin curve on a southern Ohio country road instead of sitting parked on a neighborhood street in Columbus. She was dressed professionally, in a lightweight gray jacket and skirt with a white blouse. As if she'd ditched her robe and come directly from chambers.

At last she said, "I need your help."

"OK. With what?"

"I'm in trouble."

"I'm sorry to hear that. What kind?"

"It's . . ."

"Is it the campaign?"

She didn't respond right away. Eons passed as one-celled organisms floating in primordial soup evolved, took to the land, built civilizations, made love and war, invented streaming TV, declined, and went extinct. The bird in the tree stopped singing.

"It's not the campaign," she said. "At least not directly. But I'm in a bind and I didn't know who else to call. I hope you don't mind."

"Why would I mind?"

A nervous laugh. "We didn't exactly part on the best of terms, if you recall."

I studied her profile, the set of her jaw and the look of concentration as she stared down my street in German Village. Smelled her perfume. Realized she was wearing contacts, not the glasses I was accustomed to. But that's what happens when the only time you spend with someone is Sunday mornings in a condo with the curtains drawn and it's next stop: bedroom.

"I'll take the blame for that," I said. "I was the one who broke things off. Remember?"

"Oh, I remember. You blindsided me, that's for sure. Bringing back such lovely memories of Paul. But maybe it was for the best, in the long run."

"I'm sorry—"

"Skip it, Andy. That's not why I'm here. I'm a big girl. That's in the past now."

"Is it?"

A shadow fell over her face as she wrestled with her thoughts. I'd seen that look before, but not in the bedroom. "The Velvet Fist," they called her at the courthouse, though not to her face. Fair but tough. A judge who called them like she saw them. It was on the strength of that reputation she was running for a seat on the Ohio Supreme Court, and, according to everything I'd heard and read, had a decent shot at winning this fall.

"Laura—"

"I said skip it. I'm in trouble, real trouble, and I need your help."

"I'm listening."

"Please do, for both our sakes."

In hindsight, Laura's and my time together marked one of the stranger episodes in my life. She was a judge on the county common pleas court who earned her nickname handing down long prison sentences, especially to defendants convicted of violent offenses. I'm a private investigator who does a little security on the side. We met at a Christmas party hosted by my sometime boss, defense attorney Burke Cunningham, almost seven years ago. Two days after the party, Laura called me out of the blue with a job offer. She needed a bodyguard. She'd had threats from the brother of a gangbanger she put behind bars for life plus fifty years. The pay was good and the assignment simple enough: drive her to the courthouse each morning and back to her condo each afternoon. She preferred a private guy like me as opposed to the sheriff's office security detail because she didn't want hints of her vulnerability bandied around the gossipy legal community. Two weeks passed without incident. Then one cold January afternoon she asked me inside on the pretense of checking the alarm system. In a matter of minutes my assignment evolved into bodyguard with benefits. She canceled my contract and we started our relationship.

Such as it was. By mutual agreement I called on her once a week. Sunday mornings at 11:30 a.m. sharp, rain or shine, brunch plans or otherwise, to meet her physical needs after a bitter divorce that left her wary of anything smacking of commitment. Letting myself in with a loaned key. The confidential situation suited both of us just fine for a month of Sundays and then some. I knew enough not to bring up the cases in her courtroom, despite the fact they were often subject to stories in the *Columbus Dispatch*. If she knew anything about my pre–private

3

eye background, she never mentioned it, up to and including my fall from grace as an Ohio State quarterback and short stint with the Cleveland Browns. We kept the small talk to the weather and Columbus traffic and focused mostly on shedding our clothes as quickly as possible.

Then came the day I suggested dinner out. From Laura's reaction you would have thought I'd proposed prancing naked together through the lobby of the Franklin County Courthouse at lunchtime. So I broke it off. Strings-free sex sounds good until you're staring into a bachelorhood future with only slightly more days ahead than behind and growing tired of always going to movies alone.

Although come to think of it, I'm still a bachelor and most of the time just stay in and watch Netflix.

Laura's reaction to my breakup was resolute: I hadn't seen or spoken to her for nearly five years. Until my phone buzzed that morning and I answered and she asked if she could see me as soon as possible. I asked if she wanted me to meet her at her condo—I knew the way, after all. She said no, that she'd swing by my house. And then after a pause asked for directions.

I shoved away the memories and looked at her.

"Go ahead."

She pushed a strand of thick, dark hair off her patrician brow, and for the first time since I arrived steadied her eyes, the color of a clear sky in January, directly on mine. I swallowed, taking in her perfume, recalling Sunday mornings.

"Before I say anything else, I need you to promise me something."

"If I can."

"If you can?"

"Just being honest. I can promise a lot of things—discretion, protection, my signature on a souvenir football jersey if I'm in a really good mood. But I can't promise to break the law or over-look a crime or drink any cocktail with cucumber involved. I live by a code."

"Andy, I'm serious."

"Same goes for cilantro—"

"*Andy.*"

I apologized. Told her I defaulted to jokes because I was nervous seeing her again.

"Me too," she said.

"Take your time. Whenever you're ready."

She took a breath. "I'm ready."

"In that case, so am I."

We were in each other's arms almost before I realized what was happening. Her mouth was on mine, urgent, her lips as soft as I remembered them. I cupped my left hand around her neck and pulled her closer. We kissed like that for almost a minute, passion growing as long-dormant memories of our Sunday mornings surfaced. She murmured something and I reached under the hem of her blouse and pushed my left hand onto her cool skin. She gasped but didn't resist. It was like being in middle school again, except in a Lexus.

"Let's go inside," I whispered. "What will the neighbors think?"

"Yes," she said, her breath warm on my cheek.

And then her phone went off.

In fairness, I'm as culpable as the next guy when it comes to disruptive ring tones. My current flavor of the month, "Welcome to the Jungle" by Guns N' Roses, was not exactly soothing. But that was a harp version of Pachelbel's Canon in D compared to her abrasive, old-fashioned telephone jangle, as jarring at that moment as if someone had rolled down the window and dashed a bucket of ice water on us.

"Shit," she said, pulling away. "*Sorry.*" She fumbled for her purse and pulled out the offending device. I glanced at the screen and glimpsed a caller ID photo of a man I didn't recognize: angular face, dark hair, forced smile.

"Hi," she said. Several seconds passed. "What? *What?* My God—are you all right?" She glanced over at me. Our eyes locked, just for a moment, before she turned away. "No, don't do that. Just stay there. I'll be right over. No. *No.* I'm not sure. Maybe fifteen minutes. You're sure you're OK? All right. I will. OK—goodbye."

She disconnected the call and dropped the phone in her purse.

"I need to go."

"Go where? Who was that?"

She hesitated. "I apologize, Andy. Maybe this was a mistake."

"A mistake? What are you talking about?"

"I can't—"

"Laura, what's going on? That didn't sound good."

"Please. I have to go." She glanced at her watch. "I just need a little time. Maybe then I can explain everything."

"Should we be calling the police? If this is something to do with being a judge, with a case, you can't take any risks."

"No—no police."

"Why not?"

"I can't tell you. And I really need to go."

"Do you want me to come with you?"

She hesitated again, wrestling with her thoughts once more. The Velvet Fist, deep in contemplation. I sat back in my seat. Considered my options. Thought about where this ranked on the list of strange dates I'd been on. Decided it was top five, and that included the time I was subpoenaed in flagrante delicto.

After a few seconds she shook her head. "Give me an hour. Just to make sure everything's OK. Will you still be home, if I come back then? I'm really sorry—"

"Nothing to be sorry about, if you're sure. And yes, I'll be home. I promised Hopalong we could watch *Homeward Bound* again."

"Thanks," she said, oblivious to the joke. She looked at her phone as if expecting it to ring once more. "And yes, I'm sure. I won't be long, promise."

"That's fine. But just in case, do you have a dollar?"

"What?"

"You heard me. A bill, preferably, but I'd take one of the Susan B. Anthony coins, too."

"Andy, please. I've got to get—"

"Just a dollar."

Puzzlement filled her face as she stared at me. I didn't look away. Sighing deeply, she dug into her purse, pulled out a wallet, opened it, and retrieved a bill. "I'm really not sure why you're—"

"Thank you," I said, tucking it into my shirt pocket. "I'm considering that my retainer. I'm officially working for you now, which means I'll need your permission before I can tell anyone about our conversation."

That almost won a smile. She opened her mouth as if to say something, then closed it at the sound of a ping from her purse. She reached in, picked up her phone, looked at the screen, and tightened her lips. What I saw next on her face startled me: it was pure fear.

I said, "It's not too late to change your mind—I could still come along."

"Thanks, but no thanks. I'll see you soon."

"In that case I'll be here. With the dollar."

She didn't respond as I opened the door and climbed out. I waited just a moment, but she gave a little shake of her head. Reluctantly, I shut the door, and two seconds later she drove off. She paused briefly at the stop sign at Whittier, rolled through, and was gone.

2

AFTER A FEW SECONDS of fruitless staring down the street, I trudged up the walk to my house at 837 Mohawk. I was opening the door when I heard an engine roaring to life. I looked and saw a van leaving the curb a block down a little too quickly and heading in the same direction as the judge's Lexus. It too rolled through the stop sign and was gone. I stared a moment longer before walking inside.

I stomped to the rear, opened the door, and let Hopalong out into my postage stamp of a backyard. I refilled his water bowl, pulled a Black Label from the fridge, opened it, drained it in less time than it takes a jury to file in with its verdict, and grabbed another beer. I sat down at my kitchen table, started up my laptop, stood up and let the dog in, sat back down, and Googled Franklin County judge Laura Porter.

For the next few minutes I studied the results, trying but failing to see anything that might explain what just happened. So far as I could tell, the Web hits were divided evenly between media accounts of cases she oversaw and references to her Supreme Court campaign against William O'Malley, an appeals court judge from Youngstown. The former links were the usual grab bag of activity that passes through any big city judge's courtroom. A murder here, a burglary there: an environmental land dispute, an attempted murder, a medical malpractice claim. But as I scrolled down, one of the criminal cases caught my attention.

WOMAN ARRESTED AFTER THREATENING JUDGE AT SENTENCING

Six weeks ago, Laura sent a nineteen-year-old man to prison for sixty-three years for wounding a child in a drive-by shooting that left the boy permanently paralyzed. The defendant was black, as was the child, who was just seven years old. Immediately afterward, the man's mother stood up and called Porter a bitch who hates black people. At her instruction, deputies dragged the woman out of the courtroom. She was charged with inducing panic and contempt of court. I wrote the woman's name down. Could this be the problem?

I'm in trouble . . . My God—are you all right?

Whose call was it that ended our impassioned fumbling and flipped her switch so completely? Whose photo was on the caller ID I glimpsed? A family member? A lover? Someone from the courthouse? What was the subsequent text that scared Laura so? And was it my imagination, or had the van that pulled out moments after she left seemed in a bit of a hurry for a lazy late summer evening?

I turned to the campaign web links. Unlike most political races, judicial competitions are normally about as exciting as watching Sherwin-Williams samples dry. Codes of conduct prevent a lot of the normal mudslinging. Third-party groups can get involved, pouring in unrestricted funds from the left and the right, but so far this had been a relatively uneventful face-off. Laura, a moderate Republican, had a small lead in the one and only poll taken so far. O'Malley, a Democrat, seemed a decent enough guy, and you couldn't entirely write off his chances, if only because of his name. In Ohio as elsewhere, judges with Irish surnames earned an instant advantage in campaigns. His only blemish was a decade-old incident in which he admitted cheating on the number of hours he recorded for his continuing education classes. He blamed the mistake on procrastination brought on by stress. A professional conduct board cleared him of wrongdoing. Small potatoes in the world of political scandals, and it was unclear if voters cared—or even knew there was a campaign on and who the candidates were. At this point, it was probably Laura's race to lose.

I threw in the towel after an hour. Whatever trouble Laura was in, it wasn't in the public record or related to the race, so far as I could see. I opened the front door and glanced up and down the street. No sign of her Lexus, or a van in a hurry. I took a third Black Label into the living room, picked up my copy of *Glass House,* and started reading, checking the time every few minutes or so.

Everything OK? I texted when two hours had passed. No response. Half an hour later I tried calling, but got only voice mail. The greeting unchanged after all this time: "Hi, it's Laura. You know the drill." I didn't bother leaving a message. Unease growing, I went back to my book, reading until my eyes started to droop, which was right around the time Hopalong was scratching the back door for one last trip outside. I sent a final text before heading to bed:

Come by no matter what time.

My phone stayed silent.

I'VE PASSED MORE RESTFUL nights in jail cells ahead of arraignments. When I awoke shortly after six o'clock, feeling as exhausted as when my head hit the pillow, the first thing I did was pick up my phone. My heart skipped a beat. There was a missed call from Laura shortly before midnight which somehow I'd slept through. A call, but no message. Sitting up, still half asleep, I pressed redial but once again got only voice mail.

This time I left a message, hung up, and tried again immediately. Same result. I debated what to do, though I knew within seconds there was only one choice, as dramatic as it seemed. Because something was wrong. The trouble she said she was in. The strange call: *My God—are you all right?* The van pulling away from the curb, fast. Her promise to return, followed by radio silence, followed by a call but no voice mail.

Fifteen minutes later, shaved and clutching a travel mug of coffee, I was in my Honda Odyssey headed north to her condo in an upscale faux–English cottage development off Dublin Road on the northwest side. The place she bought after the divorce occasioned by her husband's declaration at breakfast one morning that he was leaving her for an associate at his blue-chip downtown law firm. The other woman only a bit older than half Laura's age. A declaration—from the little I knew of the event—as unexpected as a blow to the head with a two-by-four. How had Laura put it, referring to the day I dumped her? *You blindsided me, that's for sure. Bringing back such lovely memories of Paul.*

Twenty minutes later I parked, checked my surroundings, walked to the door, and rang the bell. I studied my phone while I waited, one of the most surefire and also most misleading ways to convince people you don't pose a threat. I rang a second time, and then after thirty seconds rapped the metal knocker. Nothing. I tried the door handle. Locked. Looking around, I reached into my pocket, pulled out a key, and inserted it in the lock.

Call it a hazard of my trade. Call it deviousness. Call it a safeguard against my penchant for misplacing things. Go with a combo meal, if you like. For whatever reason, I guarded the key Laura had given me back in the day carefully. So carefully that I disobeyed her instructions and made a copy anyway. Which, for reasons I couldn't explain fully, I kept in a drawer after our breakup. The fact I hadn't looked at it in five years until this morning didn't spare me a residual twinge of guilt over my—what? Breach of contract? Ethical oversight? Wishful thinking?

I recalled once more the strange call, her fear, and the suspicious van, pushed the thoughts away and turned the key. A moment later I was inside.

3

"LAURA?"

No response. The house dark except for a single lamp on an end table in the living room. I shut the door behind me, took a few steps farther in, and looked around. She'd replaced the couch with something a little higher end, and it looked as if the walls had a new coat of off-beige paint. Otherwise the house appeared the same as the one I used to visit each Sunday morning. Neat—neater than my place, anyway—but lived in. Nothing immediately suspicious. Throw pillows slightly off-kilter on the couch; TV remote resting atop a day-old *New York Times* on the coffee table; an empty wine glass beside it, bottom ringed with red. No signs of a break-in or a ransacking or anything out of the ordinary.

I stepped into the kitchen, calling her name again. Here too, things appeared normal. A coffee cup and a small plate sat in the left chamber of the double metal sink, but the counter area was clear and the surface free of finger smudges. I stepped over and examined the door of her refrigerator and the magnets she'd adorned it with. "Let's go somewhere and judge people," read one, picturing two women in brightly colored fifties-style dresses. "I'm not here to judge. I'm just here to point out your mistakes," said another, superimposed over a photo of Laura—a birthday gag gift, perhaps? And one I remembered well: "Book lovers never go to bed alone." In the middle of the magnets, the pad of narrow stationery with a wildflower design she kept affixed there for her weekly shopping list. Several items penciled in, starting with *Eggs, bananas, 1 percent milk*, the *1 percent* underlined. So Laura, so precise. Why describe the type of milk when she was the only person drinking it?

I walked down the hall toward the bedroom. Her office was on the left. It was common back in the day for me to enter and find her at her computer in her nightgown reading legal briefs or working on a decision or checking e-mail. She'd direct me to the bedroom with a flutter of fingers on a raised right hand, often not even turning around. It was a habit—one of many— that annoyed me at the time. Now I found myself missing it as I hoped against hope to see her sitting there, just like always. But the room was empty.

Unease growing, I walked the rest of the way to the bedroom. The door was partway closed. I thought about retreating to my van and retrieving the Louisville Slugger I keep there for protection and in case of an outbreak of league softball. But time was of the essence. I took a breath and pushed the door open all the way.

"Jesus Christ!"

I stepped back, heart pounding, as a gray blur streaked past me. I turned and saw the tip of a tail round the corner into the living room. I put my hand on my chest. A cat. An addition to the house, which had been pet-free in my day. Though my family had both cats and dogs as I grew up in rural Ohio, I always preferred dogs, finding cats too aloof and uneven in their affections. But a perfect companion for Laura, I thought, stepping into the bedroom.

I half-feared finding her body splayed across the bed or lying on the floor. But this room was empty too. Her nightstand contained a stack of *New Yorker* magazines, a framed photo of her son and daughter, now young adults—I knew she doted on them, especially after the divorce—and a book of legal definitions. I picked the book up and read the cover description: "More than 3,500 legal terms defined in plain English!" Dry even by Laura's standards, I thought, setting it down. I glanced at the bed, recalling our Sundays together. It was made, of course. Many was the morning I emerged from the master bathroom to find the judge remaking the bed just minutes after we tousled the sheets, as if to erase any signs of what just happened between them. The look she gave me the one and only time I teased her about it forestalled any future comment on the practice.

I pulled out my handkerchief and spent the next couple minutes opening drawers and examining their contents. I repeated the routine with her closet, careful not to disturb any clothes. Her outfits were conservative and well-made, a mix of Talbots and Nordstrom's, with few casual options. I saw one pair of jeans, and in their own special corner, the duds she wore to the condo's workout club three mornings a week. A couple blouses lay on the floor beside a hamper, but other than that, no sign of anything out of the ordinary. Also no sign, I deduced, of a male presence in the condo.

Satisfied I hadn't missed anything, and deeply dissatisfied by what I was seeing—or not seeing—I left the bedroom and went back down the hall. I looked around and spied the cat on the far arm of the couch cleaning itself.

"What have you seen?"

It licked its fur, with no answer forthcoming.

I went back into the kitchen, the cat trailing me with a plaintive cry. I opened the door to the garage, flipped on the light switch, and stepped inside. I realized I had never been there before, and so wouldn't know what was in or out of place. On the far wall hung a neatly rolled-up hose, a stepladder, and a shovel that looked as shiny and new as the day Laura purchased it. On the back wall, closest to the condo, bare wood shelves held gardening implements, boxes of lightbulbs, and a lone toolbox. I took a last look around and stepped back into the kitchen.

And stepped right back into the garage.

The Lexus was gone.

But where? I glanced at my Timex. It was just past seven. I knew Laura liked to be in her chambers early, but this seemed prompt even for her. I took one last glance around, went back inside, sat on the couch, and thought. It was Tuesday morning. Laura called me yesterday shortly after 11 a.m., asking if we could meet. I'd been so taken aback I hadn't managed to ask any of the million questions crowding into my brain, but instead agreed right away to see her. The fact she needed directions to my house was hardly surprising given the cordoned-off nature of our relationship way back when, though it stung just a little, if I were being honest about it.

So where was she now? I wondered briefly if I'd made a colossal mistake and would have a lot of explaining to do when she opened the door any minute now, back from an early morning milk run. *1 percent,* underlined. But no, that was absurd. Laura would no sooner run out of a staple than give a wife abuser a slap on the wrist. Plus there was the missed call last night, on top of the strange call she received in the midst of our middle school antics in her car. And why had she been so adamant the police weren't to be involved? What, or who, was she so afraid of?

The cat rounded the corner, looked up at me, and cried again. I stood and glanced at matching food and water bowls on the kitchen floor. The water bowl was low. I took it and refilled it in the sink. I looked around for a bag of kibble and found it in a bottom-level cupboard. I filled the bowl and thought: this isn't right. Laura—leave her cat's food bowl empty? Not the judge I knew. I considered the empty garage and the missing Lexus.

Assuming she'd come back here last night after wherever she'd driven off to, Laura had left her condo in a hurry, I was sure of it.

But why?

4

AFTER LOCKING UP, I returned to my van and drove home. I changed into workout clothes and half-walked, half-jogged around Schiller Park with the dog for nearly forty minutes. Finished, I punched out a round of push-ups and sit-ups, stretched, took a shower and dressed, and called Laura's chambers. It was just past eight-thirty.

"It's Archie Goodwin," I said when the bailiff came on the line. "Looking for Judge Porter?"

"The judge isn't in this morning."

"Do you expect her later?"

"I can take a message. You said Archie?"

I hung up without responding and thought for a moment. I made another decision.

"Hey, Siri," I said, bringing my phone to life. "Call Burke Cunningham."

"*Calling Burke Cunningham,*" the phone replied in a chipper Australian woman's voice. I was a reluctant convert to Siri, finally spurred by, of all people, my ex-wife Crystal, my son Joe's mom. For several weeks in a row she sent me articles of people who used the artificial intelligence technology to call 911 after being rendered helpless in a car accident. "*What if you're hurt and Joe's trapped?*" I suspected she was trying to justify the number of AI gadgets she and her husband employed in their house, but in truth it came in handy from time to time. Usually when I misplaced my phone, but for legitimate driving-hands-free purposes as well.

Cunningham was my periodic boss thanks to cases he handles as one of the city's top defense lawyers and investigations he needs done now and then. Also the person whose Christmas party led to Laura's and my introduction lo those many years ago. After he answered, I told him my concerns, leaving out the heavy petting and the fact I'd been in Laura's condo. I explained she didn't seem to be at work, which worried me.

"She said she's in trouble?"

"That's right."

"Did she say what kind?"

"No. But something wasn't sitting right. I thought if you—"

"If I what?"

"Maybe you might have better luck, seeing if everything's OK."

"Why would Porter call you in the first place? Does she know you?"

"Maybe by reputation. Plus, we met at your Christmas party."

He didn't know about Laura's and my extracurricular activities, and I decided this wasn't the best time to bring them up.

"I'll make a couple calls. It's a little strange, I agree. Maybe something with the campaign got under her skin. These high-court races are boring as hell, but the stakes are big."

An hour passed. I tried the judge's cell phone again, to no avail. I checked my e-mail. I took a couple calls for possible jobs. My other son, Mike, texted about our outing later that morning. I told him I was looking forward to it. Finally, around ten, Cunningham called me back.

"Far as I can tell the judge called in sick today. Not a big deal, since her docket was light. An arraignment that the prosecutor agreed to continue a day and a status conference on a civil suit. She's probably just taking it easy at home."

"I don't think that's the case."

"What do you mean?"

I hesitated. "I've been to her condo. She's not there. And her car's gone."

"You went to her house?"

I acknowledged it.

"You went *inside*?"

"Something like that."

"Please don't tell me you broke in. Because that opens up a whole can of—"

"I have a key."

"You have a key to Judge Porter's condo? Why?"

"It's a long story."

"I look forward to hearing it. Just hopefully not in a deposition. OK, stay put, will you?"

He called again in fifteen minutes.

"I need you to run downtown. The sheriff's office wants to talk to you."

"Me? Why?"

"I'm sorry, Andy. I had to tell someone. I'm a lawyer, which makes me an officer of the court. If a judge is in trouble, and I'm aware of it, it's my duty to alert authorities. It sounds like it's probably just a misunderstanding. But just in case, do you mind—?"

And so it was that a few minutes later I found myself in a conference room on the fourth floor of the Franklin County sheriff's office on South High on the other side of the street from the county justice department, seated across a table from a stone-faced detective named Chad Pinney.

"This had better be good," he said. "This is supposed to be my day off."

"Must be nice," I said.

"Strike one. Start talking."

5

I BEGAN WITH HEARING from her the previous day, proceeded to my conversation with the judge in her car, the call that interrupted our moment together—as with Burke, I left out the details of what we were doing just then—the fear on her face and my concerns someone in a van was keeping an eye on her, the discovery of the missed call hours later, and then, most precariously, my walk through her condo and the strange detail that her car was gone.

"First things first," Pinney said. "How is it you were inside the judge's house?"

"I have a key."

"I gathered that. But why?"

My mind raced, trying to decide if Laura would be more upset at the disclosure of an unorthodox romantic relationship or an end-run around the powers that be at the courthouse. With no receivers to pass to on my left or my right, I decided to cradle the ball and run straight up the middle.

"I do some security consulting on the side. A while back the judge asked me to take a look at her condo, do some measuring and some surveillance. She couldn't always be there. So—"

"So she gave you a key?"

"She said it was easier that way."

"Easier than what?"

"Than her always having to be there, when I was working."

"And you still have it? The key?"

Carefully, I said, "She wanted me to have it. In case my services were ever needed again."

"I find that hard to believe."

"I'm sorry about that."

"I beg your pardon?"

"This is not about the key, all right? I'm worried that something's happened to the judge. It's not like I'm hiding anything."

"That's up to me to decide. Especially given your record."

"What's that got to do with anything? I'm a licensed private investigator in good standing—"

"You're a convicted criminal. I could care less what you do now. So let's just get something straight here. You don't really have any evidence that she's in danger."

I fumed, hoping the blood from biting my tongue wouldn't splash both of us. Considered reminding him—as I was often forced to in this town—that I'd served my time and was considered a rehabilitated individual in the eyes of the law. I watched Pinney watching me. Hoping I'd lose it?

I decided not to take the bait. I calmed myself down, took a breath, and explained about the cat's food bowl. He looked at me skeptically.

"I'm supposed to bother the judge on her sick day because you broke into her condo, saw that her cat's bowl was empty, and now have this feeling something's wrong?"

"I didn't break in. I told you, I have a key."

"Just answer the question."

"All that, plus our conversation last night. And the van."

"She said she was in trouble, according to you. Not danger—trouble. That could mean anything, right? Money trouble, car trouble, husband trouble. Though why she'd stoop to calling you for help with any of that is beyond—"

"She's divorced, for starters. And that kind of trouble—it's not the impression I got. And then the call she got while we were—"

"While you were what?"

"While we were talking. Everything changed. And then there's the missed call last night. How do you explain that?"

"How about a pocket dial? Ever consider that? I get two a week from my mom, easy." Pinney was heavyset, five ten or eleven, with short black hair that matched his black goatee, wearing jeans, a Franklin County Dive Team T-shirt, and an increasingly annoyed expression.

"The judge doesn't seem the pocket dial kind of person."

"So now you're a psychologist on top of a security consultant?"

"Sticks and stones, detective. All I'm suggesting is that she could be in trouble. She's had threats in her courtroom. Just a few weeks ago—"

"Trouble, according to you, and no one else."

"Yes, but—"

He interrupted before I could finish. "Listen up. I'm going to make a couple of calls, mainly to cover my ass with my supervisor, not because of anything you've told me. You're going to sit here and not go anywhere. Sound good?"

I nodded, though it didn't sound good at all. The detective walked out, closing the door behind him. Still annoyed at his crack about my past, I looked around the room for some kind of consolation. I was rewarded with gray walls the color of dryer lint and an off-kilter photograph of the county commissioners. I checked the time. Just over an hour before I had to meet Mike. I'd promised him a session of football throwing so he could show off his arm to me. Against both my better wishes and those of his mom, my other ex-wife, Kym, he'd gone out for his high school team. Now, as a rising sophomore, he was the second-best quarterback on the squad and hoping to challenge for the starting position. The media was having a field day with the concept: *Son of disgraced Ohio State star hopes to forge own gridiron glory.* I'd turned down five requests for interviews this month alone. Like

Mike needed the aggravation of his old man publicly weighing in on his prospects.

Like I needed that either.

"Well you're either really lucky or really dumb."

Pinney reentered the room, phone in one hand, cup of coffee in the other. No java for me, I noticed.

"I've been called both, sometimes in the same sentence."

"I bet you have. We'll go with lucky, since the judge says she's not pressing charges."

"What?"

"You heard me. She's upset, to put it mildly. First, that you were in her condo without her permission. And second, that you made me bug her. She wants the key back pronto. But she's leaving it at that."

"And you know this how?"

"Because I talked to her five minutes ago."

"You did?"

"It's called detecting. I could send you some books about it."

"That won't be necessary—"

"Here." He handed me his phone.

"What's this?"

"She wants to talk to you—against my recommendation, for the record. Take it—it's dialing."

I took the phone. I held it to my ear.

"Andy?"

"Laura? Where are you?"

I ignored Pinney's frown at my use of the judge's first name.

"That's none of your business," Laura said. "I'm very upset. What were you doing in my condo? The detective said you have a key? Where did you—"

I realized from the echo on the line she was on speaker mode. I wondered the obvious: Was she alone? Or was someone paying close attention to her conversation?

"I was worried. You never came back. And then I had a missed call from you last night."

"You must be mistaken."

"I don't think so." I explained about the empty food bowl, how it had me concerned.

"You didn't answer my question about the key."

"And you didn't explain about the cat."

"Don't be absurd, Andy. You're way out of line here."

"You don't really expect me to—"

"Listen up, Andy. Listen carefully, for a change. There's nothing going on."

"But last night. You said—"

"I was just jabbering. Forget anything I said. It's been a long month already."

Her tone was oddly strained, like someone trying to make small talk at the funeral of a younger colleague.

"Let me come see you, then. We'll have coffee."

"No. In fact, you have to promise me—"

"Promise you what?"

"Promise that you'll leave me alone."

"How can I leave you alone when I don't know where you are or what's going on?"

A heavy sigh. "You know what your problem is?"

Her voice loud enough through the phone that Pinney perked up.

"What's that?" I said.

"You ask too many questions. You always have. You milk every conversation until it's dry, until you have every last bit of information about somebody. You always have to be the big bad detective, no matter who you're with or what you're doing. Frankly, it gets old. It's exhausting."

"Laura, what are you talking—"

"Stop calling me Laura. It's Judge Porter, in case you've forgotten. I'm talking about you butting into my personal business."

"Butting? You were the one who—"

"Just leave it. Stop sticking your nose where it doesn't belong."

"Laura . . . *Judge*, I—"

"Listen carefully for once, all right? You have practically zero percent feelings for anybody but yourself. You know that? So just stop interfering. I'm fine. Do you understand?"

"No."

"*Practically zero*, Andy."

"I—"

"Goodbye."

THE PHONE DISCONNECTED. THE room was quiet. The smell of Pinney's coffee drifted in my direction. Suddenly exhausted, I could have used a cup or three myself.

The detective reached for his phone. "Satisfied?"

"No."

"Oh really? Why not?"

"She said 'jabbering.'"

"What?"

"She used the word jabbering. It's not something she would say."

He looked at me in disbelief. "And you would know this how? Same reason you know she wouldn't leave her cat's bowl empty?"

"It doesn't matter. You have to believe me. Something wasn't right. What if she wasn't able to speak freely? Have you considered that?"

"Of course I did."

"And?"

"And I eliminated that as a possibility."

"How?"

"Every judge is assigned a safe phrase," Pinney said. "Something they could bring into conversation if there's a problem. Normal sounding, but specific to them."

"And she didn't use it?"

He shook his head.

"What's the phrase?"

"Like I'm going to tell you that."

I thought about protesting. But what was the point? I was as sure as I could be that not only was Laura in trouble, she was in danger. Yet what was I supposed to do? Pinney might have been a pain in the ass, but clearly he was good at his job. He had batted down every argument with cold, hard evidence. Whatever was going on with Laura, fixing it wasn't going to happen here, in this room, with the detective doubting my every word.

"All right," I said, standing. "I appreciate you listening. I've still got my concerns. But I suppose there's nothing left to do."

"You suppose right. But just for yuks, where are you going now?"

"I'm going to toss a football around for a while, I guess."

"Perfect. You do that, and leave the detecting to the real investigators."

"If I see any, I'll be sure to do so," I said, walking out of the room before he had a chance to reply.

6

"YOU'RE NOT FOLLOWING THROUGH all the way," I yelled. "Rip your arm down across your body. Like this." I arced the ball through the air to my son, who plucked it easily with a sideways catch.

"That's what I'm doing." Mike stepped back and drilled a spiral pass at me. He threw hard enough that my hands tingled as I caught the ball. But there was no denying the slight wobble as it flew over the green expanse stretching between us. He wasn't listening.

"No, you're not," I said, impatiently gunning the ball back to him, ignoring the tweak in my arm as I threw.

We were spread out on a practice field behind Worthington Kilbourne High School, just north of Columbus, a mile or so from where Mike lived with Kym, her husband, Steve, and their two kids. The August air smelled of mowed grass and fertilizer. Mike's morning practice was over. They had a scrimmage the following Friday, the first time in uniform, though they wouldn't wear pads or be allowed to tackle. Steve was convinced his stepson had the right stuff, that a college career or more was possible. Kym was skeptical—she'd been there, seen that with me. She was also worried about his health because of the new focus on concussions. I was worried about that as well; two guys I played with in Cleveland had killed themselves, and autopsies showed severe brain damage in both. I was also prone to forgetfulness, though in fairness I'd been forgetting things that didn't involve football or girls since the ripe old age of thirteen. Kym and I permitted the dream to flourish so long as Mike kept up with his studies and his piano lessons, which somewhat to my surprise he did, along with a grass-cutting service he ran with a couple of buddies. His life of camps and trainers and physical therapists was about as far as you could get from the summers I spent tossing footballs through swing tires and over fields of corn so high I couldn't see my receiving buddy on the other side. But apparently it amounted to the same thing, since the kid could throw, even if he couldn't listen.

He tried again, better this time, but his spiral still had the slightest wobble to it, like a diving falcon with a hitch in its wing. There probably weren't five coaches in Ohio who would deem the flaw worth remarking on. But the ball might as well have been rotating end on end for all I could stand it. Instead of returning the toss, I cradled the ball and crossed the field to where he stood, eyeing me like a ref he knows is delivering bad news.

"What."

"You're doing this." I imitated his follow-through, which was stopping just short of where it should go. "Which is why you're getting that wobble."

"There's no wobble."

"There is. It's subtle, but it's there. And it's going to add up."

"What do you mean?" He took a step back, crossing his muscular arms across his chest. He'd shot up in the past school year and was now an even six foot, though with my height I didn't think he was done growing yet. Between his camps, his lawn job, and the free weights in Steve's basement—weights I paid for, thank you very much—he was an impressively fit-looking kid. At the moment he was wearing shorts, socks, and practice cleats and nothing else. Out of the corner of my eye I saw two high school–age girls crossing the field in shorts and tight T-shirts, and it wasn't me they were eyeballing.

"I mean, you can get away with it at the level you're at now. It's good enough. You'll win games and you'll be in the paper and on TV." I glanced at the girls. "You'll have a lot of fans. But there's five hundred other guys your age throwing the same spiral with the same hitch, because their release is a little funky. They're all going to be in the paper too. But they're not the ones headed for the next level, because they're competing against the five guys your age who figured out how to throw without the hitch. To complete the follow-through. Those are the ones you need to worry about. If you care."

Mike didn't say anything for a few seconds. He'd seen the girls and was doing his own reconnaissance. Then he looked back at me.

"So, 1 percent?"

"What's that?"

"Five of five hundred. One percent. That's what I'm supposed to shoot for?"

"You're supposed to shoot for even less than that. I mean otherwise, what's the point?"

"Is that what you did?"

I thought back to my own high school career. Starting quarterback in the state finals as a freshman. And that was just the beginning.

"Don't worry about what I did. We all know how that ended." *Sports Illustrated* had recently included my arrest for point-shaving my senior year at Ohio State on a list of the fifty stupidest athletic mistakes of all time. I said, "Worry about where you want to go. You've got the talent to do anything you want. You just need to listen."

He uncrossed his arms and shook them out, glanced at the girls, crossed his arms again, and looked at me.

"All right. Show me what you're talking about."

I did. After that, we threw for twenty more minutes. His last five throws were textbook, rifle shots of perfectly spiraling bullets destined for the best of the YouTube highlight films.

"That's good," I said, after he nailed yet another. "Let's call it a day."

"Why?"

I jogged back to him. "You don't want to push it. You've got your engine at perfect calibration. You rev it too much and you're back to square one. Quit while you're ahead."

"You used to throw until it was so dark you could barely see the ball," he said accusingly. "Over and over and over again. Grandpa told me that."

"I'm sure he did. And you know where he was when I was icing my elbow at the kitchen table? In front of the TV with another beer. Trust me on this. A lot of times, less is more."

"Fine. If that's what gets me to 1 percent, then whatever."

"What did you say?"

He favored me with the universal my-dad's-a-doofus expression. "What *you* said, remember? Five out of five hundred. One percent. Or better yet, *less* than 1 percent. You just told me that."

"Yes, I did."

But suddenly I wasn't thinking about football any more. I was thinking about angry words flung at me an hour earlier.

You milk every conversation until it's dry.

Listen carefully for once, all right? You have practically zero percent feelings for anybody but yourself.

Practically zero, Andy.

One percent milk. Could it be—?

"I've got to go."

"Go where?" Mike said. "I thought we were having lunch."

"We were. I'm sorry. You still are." I fished into my wallet and handed him a twenty. "Something's come up."

"Like what?" He looked at the bill as if I'd deposited a dog turd on his palm.

"Like a friend who's in trouble."

"Who?"

"Nobody you know."

He shook his head and sighed. He turned and started walking away, back toward the high school.

"Wait. I'm sorry about this, Mike. It's just—"

He waved off the objection. "It's OK. You knew where Grandpa was. And I know where you are."

"Mike—"

He jogged across the field without responding, headed in the direction of two girls in shorts and tight T-shirts.

7

I DROVE FASTER THAN I should have back to Laura's condo. My suspicion might be nothing, and if that was the case, Pinney, the sheriff's detective, was right. Better to leave the detecting to the real investigators. Plus I'd have the added pleasure of knowing I'd blown off my son for no reason. But for better or worse, my conversation with Mike loosened a nagging thought in the back of my brain, like a screw with a stripped head I'd finally been able to budge. I wouldn't be able to rest until I pulled it all the way out. A few minutes later I parked once again outside Laura's condo, inserted the purloined key into the lock on her door, turned the handle, and stepped inside.

The cat materialized a couple of seconds later. I ignored it as I walked into the kitchen, approached the refrigerator, and tore the grocery list off the pad of paper affixed there with a magnet. I held it close and read. *Eggs, bananas, 1 percent milk; 1 percent* underlined. The notation that gave me pause that morning. Who gets that specific on a list only she will see? I thought about almost the same words spoken by Laura in a different order and very different context. *Practically zero, Andy.* A coincidence, or something more? Had she been trying to tell me something over the phone at the sheriff's office, send a coded message as someone listened in? I continued reading. *Carrots, oranges, yogurt. Coffee, paper towels, chicken.*

My heart sank. There was nothing here. The groupings were random, to be sure, lumping carrots with yogurt and paper towels with chicken. Even I knew those items were on opposite sides of any store. Hardly in keeping with Laura's orderly approach to things. But so what?

I read further. *Rice, wine, granola. Escarole, estoppel, endive. TP, avocados, peanut butter. Soda water, dish soap—*

I stopped. I read backwards up the list. Estoppel?

I looked closer. Was I misreading the word? Laura's handwriting wasn't the neatest in the world, but it was still a more than serviceable cursive. At second glance there was no question about it. Laura had inserted an arcane legal word I'd heard a few times but couldn't possibly have defined into the middle of her weekly grocery list. But why? I pulled out my phone and looked up a definition. *The principle that bars a person from asserting something contrary to what is implied by a previous deed or statement of that person or by a previous relevant judicial determination.* Huh? I searched for plain English definitions and after a couple minutes decided it basically meant you couldn't try to prove or disprove something in a legal argument whose truth had already been established.

Like, say, denying anything was wrong after you'd called an ex-lover out of the blue after five years and told him you were in trouble?

I folded the list, placed it in my wallet, stepped back, and leaned against the counter. The cat approached and rubbed back and forth against my legs. So Laura left behind a clue after all. But for who? Me? She'd dropped the hint during our call at the sheriff's office. But how could she have known I'd show up at her condo on the basis of one missed phone call? A darker thought crossed my mind. Maybe she hadn't been that calculating. Maybe she left a clue on her shopping list so that, no matter what happened to her, someone, someday, might be able to figure out the truth. Only by luck was I the one who earned the first shot at the puzzle.

But what was I supposed to do with this? How was I meant to handle a handwritten legal term hiding in plain sight on a grocery list like a link of German sausage nestled in a drawer of red Christmas candles? Call Detective Pinney back? *"Hey, I know this sounds a little weird, but . . ."*

I put myself in Laura's position. If I was right, she'd handed me proof that something was indeed rotten in Denmark. But so what? I'd been thinking that all day, despite her subsequent denial of a problem over the phone as Pinney eavesdropped. Laura was more calculating than that. Anyone who knew her well—and I was going to count myself in that category—knew that the "Velvet Fist" nickname was the beginning of her legal reputation, not the end. She was renowned for her deliberate and thoughtful approach to cases. I knew she prided herself on rarely being overturned on appeal.

There must be more, I thought.

I walked slowly through her apartment, seeing if anything else caught my eye. Something told me that having hidden one clue in the open, she would have done it again. No treasure boxes under loose floorboards for her. I glanced at the bookshelves on either side of her fireplace, jammed with a combination of biographies, histories of various global conflicts, and a smattering of legal thrillers. Nothing that said estoppel, and nothing that made me think her plan was for me—or someone—to pull every volume off a shelf to search.

Next I went into her office. I tried the computer, but the password protection was on. I knew someone who could help me with that if it came to it, but again I wondered. Laura would have known that checking her computer files would be a chore for whoever tackled it. The chances were good that *estoppel* appeared frequently, adding to a needle in the haystack problem. I crossed the computer off the list as an option. The desk it sat on was clear except for a couple of bills marked "paid." I tried the file drawers, but none of the folders was marked with the word of the day. I was about to walk out when I glanced in the wastepaper basket. Something didn't look right. I reached in and pulled out the offending piece of trash.

It was a black frame, 8½ by 11, its glass shattered. From the force of being thrown away? I loosened a couple of the shards and carefully tossed them back into the basket. The frame held a certificate. *The Berman Prize*. An award of some kind, I recalled, from the judge's Ohio State law school days. I'd glanced at it a dozen times during our purported romance, pausing in the office to say hello and to attempt a seductive gesture like kissing the back of Laura's neck. Usually a mistake. I wasn't sure what kind of prize it was, although I assumed, with Laura's smarts, it was an academic honor. I looked around and saw a small nail jutting out where the frame once hung to the right of her desk. For some reason Laura—or someone—had trashed the framed certificate, and not nicely. I picked out more glass shards. I thought about taking the certificate, and then remembered Pinney's skepticism about my presence in the condo. I set the remains of the frame beside Laura's computer and took a couple pictures of the certificate instead. Strange. But the source of her trouble? It seemed unlikely.

Next I returned to the bedroom. I lowered myself to my hands and knees and looked under the bed. I started as a pair of gleaming eyes stared back me. The cat, creeping about with no regard for privacy. But other than her—him?—there was nothing to see other than a dust bunny or two and an errant sock.

I rose on my knees and was about to stand when my eyes came to rest on her nightstand. The pile of *New Yorkers*. The photo of her children, who meant so much to her. The dry-as-dust book of legal definitions.

Who keeps that kind of book as bedside reading?

I grabbed it, stood up and flipped through its pages.

Ejectment, Eleventh Amendment, En Banc.

Enumerated Powers. Equitable Defense. Escape Clause.

Escrow, Estate at Sufferance, Estoppel—

A single piece of paper fluttered to the floor.

8

I LEANED OVER AND retrieved the sheet. On it were two words, in Laura's handwriting. *Mendon Woods*.

I sat on her bed and pulled out my phone again. This turned out to be an easier internet search than a definition of *estoppel* understandable by a mere mortal. According to the very first article I read, Mendon Woods was an undeveloped plot of land on the north side of town, on the far side of the outer belt from Columbus but still in the county. A mix of ordinary Ohio hardwoods, some prairie—probably not original—and at its center, a small wetland about nineteen acres in circumference. There were probably bigger Walmart parking lots than that particular swamp. Nearly all of the few hundred acres surrounded by development. And possibly not long for this world. Mendon Woods' future was up in the air because of a lawsuit brought by a developer against the state, which had jurisdiction over the property. A lawsuit on the docket of one Franklin County Common Pleas Judge Laura Porter.

THE FACTS WERE SIMPLE enough. A company called Rumford Realty wanted Mendon Woods for an unspecified commercial development. A few months back, a deal was brokered whereby the company would receive the property in exchange for mitigating the wetlands loss by creating a bigger artificial wetlands area adjacent to the Scioto River north of Columbus. The wetlands was self-contained, not reliant on a creek or river, so the state, not the feds, had jurisdiction, simplifying things. The arrangement was finished and on the way to the printer's when environmental groups blew the whistle and criticized the state for kowtowing to a businessman and destroying one of the last natural wetlands inside the county. The swamp in Mendon Woods, though tiny, was classified as category III—the richest and most diverse type. It was home to numerous animals and an important stopover for migratory birds, some of them rare, including something called a coastal tanager. A mitigated wetland, no matter how big, wasn't the same and often didn't function properly, the argument went. The state bowed under public pressure and reneged on the deal. Rumford Realty sued. The case landed in Laura's courtroom. A three-day trial ended a couple of weeks ago, with parties on both sides instructed to file final briefing documents. The judge was supposed to rule soon.

Was this the trouble Laura was in? Something to do with this swamp? All types of possibilities crossed my mind. A bribe on the table from Rumford? A threat from the environmentalists? Vice versa? Or maybe a mistake Laura made that could blow up in her face? Affect her Supreme Court campaign somehow?

I thought about texting her, asking her about the case. In the end I decided not to. There was no question in my mind now that when I spoke to her in the sheriff's office something wasn't right. The clues she dropped in the conversation led me to the book of legal definitions and this lawsuit. True, she didn't use her safe phrase with Pinney. But maybe that was an act of self-preservation forced on her by someone. I thought again about calling Pinney back, and again decided against it. I was as sure as I've been of anything that Laura was in trouble, and that the mysteriously telegraphed messages leading to the words *Mendon Woods* on a scrap of paper in a legal definition book were prime evidence of the fact. But it was also true that Laura's involvement in the case was hardly a secret, and it was semi-plausible that that scrap of paper with those words could have been a handy bookmark.

The cat appeared, jumping on my lap. I pushed it aside, stood up, pocketed the paper, and made my third big decision of the day. According to the clue—if indeed it was such a thing—answers about Laura's troubles led from here to a swamp on the north side of town. That would be my next stop. But first I needed to know more about Rumford Realty and the case before Laura. I instructed Siri to call Bonnie Deckard. She answered after one ring.

"Hey, Andy."

"Am I catching you at a bad time?"

"Just on the way to the gym. What's up?"

"You must be feeling better."

"I'm not barfing as much, if that's what you mean."

"That's not exactly how I would have put it. But that's good to hear. How's your schedule looking? I need a little research."

"Am I breaking any laws this time?"

"Not that I'm aware of—for the time being, anyway."

"Probably for the best, given everything, you know?"

Bonnie was a freelance Web designer and IT consultant. She also took on occasional jobs for me, either when a technological puzzle surpassed my abilities—meaning most of the time—or when I was in a hurry like now. Bonnie possessed three things I'd come to prize in a case consultant: efficiency, speed, and powerful enough encryption software that she could occasionally cross certain lines safely and clandestinely. When she wasn't inhabiting the world of ones and zeroes, she was a blocker on Columbus's Roller Derby team, the Arch City Roller Girls. Not long ago, that would have explained her midday jaunt to the gym. But she'd recently learned she was expecting, with twins at that, and so was spending less time on burpees, leg presses, and the elliptical machine and more on yoga and swimming. And not crossing certain lines, apparently.

I explained what I needed her to do with Rumford Realty and the case before Laura.

"I'll poke around when I get back. By the way, any chance you could take Troy out for a beer this week?"

"I'm always up for beer. Why?"

"He's still struggling a bit with the whole baby thing. Babies, I mean. I figured talking to another dad might help."

"You mean any other dad but me?"

"He looks up to you, Andy. You know that."

Bonnie's boyfriend and I had a complicated history, but I was happy to do a favor for Bonnie given how much she helped me out, and told her so.

Disconnecting, I left Laura's bedroom and walked down the hall. I was about to exit the apartment when the cat appeared and brushed against my legs. I recalled the empty food bowl. It wouldn't be like Laura to leave the cat alone without making arrangements. Was this another indication the judge was incapacitated?

Either way, I knew I couldn't leave the cat there. By taking it, the worst that could happen was Laura would reappear later that day and demand to know where her pet was. Leaving it, the worst that could happen didn't bear thinking about. I just hoped Hopalong was up for the company.

With the cat watching me from the counter, I shuttled its food dishes and litter box out to my van. Back inside, I borrowed a towel from Laura's bathroom, snared the protesting cat, wrapped the towel around it and walked outside. I went back in for a final look around. By the door to the garage I spied an extra set of Laura's keys hanging on a hook. House and Lexus, including a spare fob. What the heck, I thought. In for an inch. I pocketed the keys, locked up the condo and headed home. Once again I pushed the speed limit. I couldn't get over the feeling that time was running out.

9

I PUT THE CAT'S food bowl and water dish on my kitchen counter, out of reach of Hopalong's vacuum-like appetite. The cat's back went up immediately when it spied the dog, whereas the Lab spent all of twenty seconds staring at it curiously before retreating to the couch. So hopefully there would be something left of my house when I returned.

Thirty minutes later I was pulling into a gravel parking lot framed by weathered split-rail logs half a mile off Sawmill Road on the northwest side. Even with a stand of maples lining the entrance behind me it was still possible to see the orange corner of a Home Depot a few hundred yards away. The rush of traffic on Sawmill was distinct, like an incessant breeze, and a smell of cooked meat wafted in from a nearby McDonald's. A wilderness this was not. This was a petunia in an onion patch operated by an agribusiness. Just standing there glancing at the trees ahead of me, I could understand both sides' arguments. For a developer, this acreage was a lost cause whose fate was being sealed by the growth around it one load of hot, steaming asphalt at a time. Why not call it a day, especially since the world would get an even bigger swamp in return? For an environmentalist, these fields and forest were a last stand whose fate would determine how society dealt with nature on the brink. Why not save it, since no one could plausibly argue the world needed one more strip plaza anchored by a Starbucks on one end and a Verizon store on the other? I didn't envy Laura her decision.

I followed a packed dirt trail through the woods, noticing how the sounds of the outside world diminished the farther I walked, traffic noise dimming just a little and the smell of frying meat gone altogether, replaced by a mossy, wet odor that took me back to patches of forest on my uncle's farm that my sister and I explored for hours as kids. After ten minutes of steady hiking I stepped onto an elevated boardwalk at a break in the woods. I read a marker that explained the biological diversity present in the swamp ahead of me. Herons, cranes, and hawks hunted there. Numerous songbirds called it home, including the coastal tanager, a Brazilian native that migrated north and summered in the few remaining swamplands that it favored. I looked up, hoping to glimpse the bird, but detected only a flutter of wings that could have been anything from a sparrow to a mourning dove.

I walked along the boardwalk toward the swamp. Just as I fostered the fantasy of seeing Laura in her home office when I entered her condo that morning, I imagined seeing the judge round the corner ahead of me, a smile on her face as she congratulated herself on luring me to a romantic rendezvous with a clever collection of verbal and handwritten clues. But no one was there. I walked another hundred yards until the walkway ended at an expanded platform overlooking a small pond at the heart of the park.

I put my hands on the rail running around the platform and gazed over the water, which was dark and brackish, its edges coated with algae like brushstrokes of undulating green batter. At my approach sunning frogs catapulted themselves into the water with a pitter-patter of splashes. Below me a mud-brown water snake glided into the depths in pursuit of lunch. On the far side of the pond a small stand of reeds was encroaching into the water. Something in the middle caught my eye. What I'd first mistaken for another pair of reeds were the legs of a heron. The bird stood motionless at the edge of the plants, head slightly lowered. I looked closer and saw just a few feet away another frog, this one sitting atop a lily pad, facing the opposite way, oblivious to the danger directly behind it. The heron extended its neck almost imperceptibly, raised a stick-like leg, and advanced noiselessly a few inches in the water. The frog didn't move. I was torn between clapping my hands and giving the little guy a chance and doing nothing and watching the circle of life unfold in all its cruel efficiency. I chose the latter, for better or worse. The heron took another step, and then a sound behind me interrupted it, the creak of a loose board on the observation deck, and the frog disappeared with a splash and I turned and reflexively stepped back as the knife in the hand of a man crouching behind me bit into air instead of my rib cage.

10

HE SWORE SOFTLY, LIKE someone stubbing his toe in church, and jumped toward me, knife flashing at my neck. I pivoted out of reach and scrambled to my left. The move left him off balance, and in the moment he needed to regain equilibrium I made a fist and swung it down hard on his knife hand. He grunted in pain and staggered backward but kept his grip on the weapon.

"What the—" I managed, eyes still on the knife, which meant I didn't see his left hand as it shot out and grabbed me by the throat. He was shorter than me, thin and wiry, and in a fair fight I might have come out on top. At least that's what I told myself as he tightened vice-like fingers until I started to gasp, unable to dislodge him. Unable to stop him from swinging the knife down and under, straight for my stomach. I raised my right knee and deflected the blade at the last moment. I gasped at the pain as the tip slid off my kneecap, then brought my right foot down hard on his left. He swore again and stumbled backward. I grabbed his knife hand with both of mine and squeezed his wrist. I stared at his face, up close now, taking in pale skin, watery hazel eyes, and a dark fleck just above his right cheek. He grunted, spit in my face, and, before I had time to register my discontent, headbutted me hard. I fell back, still clinging to his knife hand, and we both went down, rolling back and forth on the boardwalk like alligators in a death struggle above a real southern swamp.

Struggling for an upper hand, I grasped at his jeans, found a hole in his back pocket, and pulled, but gained nothing as the pocket tore open and my hand flung free. We rolled right and he flipped me beneath him. He won the point but lost the round as I forced his wrist against the hard edge of a supporting post jutting out of the pond and pushed with all my strength. At last he cried out in pain and his grip loosened and the knife slipped onto the deck. He reached around for it, but I got there first and pushed it over the edge. It made no more noise falling into the water than a duck disappearing below the surface after a water bug. I exhaled and was rewarded with a punch, then another, then both his hands around my neck. I raised my hands to break the grip, to find any purchase at all, but gray mist clouded my vision as I struggled to breathe. As I stared into his face, his eyes greedy with dark victory, I realized too late the fleck below his eye wasn't mud. It was a tattoo. A tear drop—the prison emblem marking the inmate as a man who has killed. Absorbing this truth, I arched my back, trying to weaken his angle. But it was too late. He had me, and behind me was a swampy pond I might soon be floating in permanently—

"Hey!"

A voice, behind us. Tear Drop paused, his grip loosening for just a second. Just long enough. I tore his hands off my neck and rolled free, gasping like a man waking from a nightmare at dawn.

"What's going on?"

A woman's voice, back on the boardwalk.

I scooted farther away, saw something on the wooden deck in front of me, and swept it up with my left hand just as Tear Drop saw what I'd done. He dashed toward me as the woman called again, nearer now. He stopped. I backed myself into a viewing bench on the side of the observation deck, gently rubbed my bruised throat with my right, and tried to stand. Tear Drop glared at me, straightened, and stared at the figure approaching from behind. He turned back toward me. His eyes were no longer greedy. Now they gleamed with disappointment, and something more. I recognized it after a moment. The hunger of a hunter who still has to eat.

"You're dead," he said, and turned and ran.

11

"ARE YOU ALL RIGHT?"

"I'm fine."

"Fine? You can't even stand up. Who was that? What's going on?"

I tried to disprove the statement by standing. Mistake.

"Fellow birder," I said, taking a breath. "We were having an ornithological dispute."

"Bullshit. I'm calling the police."

"Please don't."

"Why not?"

"Just give me a minute, OK?"

She was midthirties, with short brown hair and glasses, wearing the olive-green uniform of a park employee of some kind. She helped me to my feet and sat me on the bench. She pulled a water bottle from someplace, let me drink, then splashed the remainder on her hands and wiped my face with her fingers.

"So," she said. "Police?"

"Not yet."

"Why?" She took a step back. "Are you the bad guy here?"

"Not that I know of."

"Then why wait?"

"I need to look at something."

"Like what?"

Without replying I opened my left hand. In it sat Tear Drop's wallet, which fell onto the observation deck after I tore open his pants pocket. So at least that was something.

HER NAME WAS DEANNA Fleischer. She was a state wildlife biologist with a wetlands specialty. I knew this because she told me, but also because she handed me her card, after I handed her mine.

"What's a private detective doing in Mendon Woods?" she said, suspicion back in her eyes. "Whose side are you on?"

"Side?"

"The lawsuit?"

"Neither, as far as I know. Also, I'm an investigator, not a detective."

"In that case, what are you investigating? And who was that?"

"I don't know. I came up here on a job and he attacked me." I decided not to mention the knife. That might override my lack of interest in involving the police.

"What kind of job?"

"I can't tell you."

"Why not?"

"Because I don't really know what it is."

"You're not making much sense. Are you sure you're all right?"

"Right as rain," I said, doubtfully.

"So why not call the police?"

"I don't have time."

"Don't have time? What's the big hurry?"

I didn't respond. I was preoccupied now, going through the contents of the blue nylon wallet. There wasn't much. A little money, mostly ones and fives, and a lone receipt from the day before from Down Home Buffet, a country-cooking restaurant in a place called Mohican Township whose phone number indicated it was closer to Cleveland than Columbus. Oddly, the wallet also held two driver's licenses. The first belonged to Tear Drop, who apparently was someone named Gary Phipps of Springfield, Missouri, when he wasn't a knife-wielding would-be assassin.

The second license belonged to Laura M. Porter.

"YOU'RE SURE YOU'RE OK to drive?"

"Pretty sure."

"Pretty sure?" Fleischer asked. "Maybe you should get yourself checked out first."

"I keep aspirin in my van. And some superhero bandages from when my kids were little. The Spiderman ones usually do the trick."

We were back in the parking lot after a slower-than-normal walk up the trail. She had agreed, reluctantly, not to call the police, at least not right then.

"I've never heard of a private eye driving a Honda Odyssey," she said. "My husband always says they look like they've got a big butt."

"What can I say? My Karmann Ghia's in the shop. Plus you wouldn't believe the gas mileage. And you can fit a decent-sized magnifying glass in the glove compartment."

"Where are you going now?"

"I guess I'm going to find some country cooking." I explained about the receipt. "I'm overdue for some biscuits and gravy."

"Isn't that a bit, I don't know, dangerous?"

"Maybe. But my cholesterol's pretty decent. I eat a lot of fruit and vegetables—"

"I mean just going up there, without any idea who that guy is or what's going on?"

"It's what I do, I guess. And it beats finding lost puppies. Usually."

"I hope you're right. And I hope your job works out, whatever it is."

"Me too."

I opened the door to the van. I stopped and turned around.

"Thanks."

"For what?"

"For showing up when you did."

"My pleasure, I guess."

"Mine too. Because there's a good chance I would have been fish food if you hadn't stopped by."

12

I PULLED OUT OF the parking lot, returned to Saw-mill, drove up the road, and took the entrance onto 270. I followed it to I-71 and joined the traffic headed north, busy even on a weekday. As I traveled I pondered the obvious question: Why had Tear Drop, aka Gary Phipps, attacked me? What connection did he have to the judge? And how had he found me at the pond? I recalled the van parked behind Laura and me last night. Odds were even that whoever he was, he'd been following Laura yesterday and followed me today. And planned to eliminate me, which meant the stakes—whatever they were—were even higher than I realized at first.

Twenty minutes on I stopped at Wendy's in Sunbury for a couple of hamburgers and coffee. Back in the van, hunger sated and the ache in my head diminishing, I called Bonnie. She picked up on the third ring.

"I thought you were at the gym. I was going to leave a message."

"I had to stop."

"Everything OK?"

"I got tired. Plus I'm starving."

"Time for some pickles and ice cream?"

"Gross. I'm going to New Harvest Cafe. I love their food."

"Me too. And I'm not even pregnant." The soul food joint off Cleveland Ave was down the road from Bonnie and Troy's house in North Linden.

"Anne too," Bonnie said.

"What?"

"I'm meeting Anne there. She loves their food too."

"Great," I said, unclenching my jaw.

My ex-girlfriend, Anne Cooper, had an annoying habit of staying friends with a lot of people we both knew even after our breakup. She and I dated following the end of things with Laura, and I prided myself on maintaining an actual grown-up relationship for a change. Until Anne dumped me, pointing out that missed dates, a chronic failure to communicate, and my hand-to-mouth existence weren't necessarily all that adult. Even now, there were times when I thought of her and—

I shook my head. I'd been beaten up enough already today.

"Tell her I said hi." That obstacle surmounted, I asked Bonnie to add Gary Phipps from Springfield, Missouri, to her research. I asked her to pay special attention to any connection she might uncover linking him with Rumford Realty or Mendon Woods or Judge Laura Porter. She said she'd do what she could.

Next, I called the two Kevins. That is to say, I called Kevin McGovern, who lives one street over on Beck in our German Village neighborhood with his husband, Kevin Hessler, and their two pugs. Over the years we've traded dog-sitting duties, for their part when they're both out of town on business, and for me on days—and nights—I end up stuck on a stakeout of a straying spouse or a guy claiming workers' comp for a back injury that hasn't stopped him schlepping landscaping stones from his truck to his garden. The kind of no-deadline jobs that drive girlfriends crazy. I explained I had to make an unexpected trip out of town and might need to enlist their help, which also included feeding a stray cat.

"Not a problem." Kevin said. "Everything all right?"

"That's what I'm hoping to find out. I shouldn't be gone long. Maybe even back tonight." Even as I said it I wondered if that were true, or if I even knew what I expected to find farther north.

"Take as long as you need. Plan to come by for dinner when you're back. Kevin got a new smoker he's dying to try."

"It's a date."

The rest of the drive passed in a blur of tall cornfields on either side of me, stretches of forest, interchanges offering identical fast food and gasoline options, and dueling single and double tractor-trailer rigs jostling for position back and forth on the three lanes of Interstate 71. I thought briefly of the wildlife biologist's question. *Isn't that a bit, I don't know, dangerous?* I considered a final call, to Otto Mulligan, a bail bondsman I know and do business with occasionally, enlisting him as backup. But no, too late now. Besides, backup for what? Another run-in with Tear Drop? Unlikely, since I planned to keep my eyes open from now on. Seeing signs for Mansfield up ahead, I pushed the speed past seventy-five, focusing on Laura and 1 percent milk and the Down Home Buffet. Because there was no question about it now. The judge was definitely in trouble. The only question was what kind, and how big.

13

HAVE YOU SEEN ME?

The flier was the first thing I noticed as I pulled open the door of the restaurant and stepped inside. The question in bold black type, above a grainy color photograph of a young man named Todd Orick, missing for the past two months. The paper pinned with thumbtacks dead center on a cork bulletin board, surrounded by business cards advertising hair cutting, log splitting, auctioneering, and more. The number for the Mohican Township police department printed below the photo, asking anyone with information on Orick's whereabouts to call.

Down Home Buffet sat half a mile from the interstate, on a two-lane road off Route 13, at the bottom of a ridge of tree-covered hills running parallel with the highway. It was a long, two-story red-plank-sided building with a peaked roof meant to summon images of a classic Ohio barn. A high school–age girl greeted me as I stepped into the restaurant. She pulled a menu from a slot on the host stand and led me into the main dining room.

"Something to drink?"

My waitress, appearing less than a minute after I was seated. My mom's age or close. Resplendent in a country frock and apron.

"Just coffee, thanks. And water."

I looked around the half full dining room. Lace curtains on the windows, real red checkerboard cloth on the tables, authentic wooden wagon wheel bolted to the far wall. A couple paint-by-numbers landscapes near the wheel, plus a copy of a painting I'd seen before—a representation of the signing of the Treaty of Greenville, which helped create the modern Ohio. Customers a mix of retirees, families, and guys that looked like they drove big rigs for a living. No sign of anyone with a tear drop on his face.

My waitress reappeared with my drinks. She set them down and pulled an order pad from the pocket of a red apron with frilly white edges. "Are you ready, dear? Buffet's $12.99, all you can eat. Or you can order off the menu."

"What kind of pie do you have?"

"Apple–Dutch apple–cherry–blackberry–lemon meringue–coconut cream–pecan–chocolate cream, and peach. Peach is real good. That's my favorite."

"Peach it is."

"À la mode?"

"Why not?"

"Anything else?"

"Sure. Ever seen this guy?"

"I'm sorry?"

I produced Tear Drop's license and handed it to her.

"Look familiar?"

She studied it for an honest five seconds or so, then placed it beside my coffee cup like a gift card to a store she'd never in a million years patronize. "Can't say that it does."

"Anybody else?"

"Anybody else what?" she said nervously.

"Would anyone else here recognize him?"

"May I ask why you're inquiring?"

I dug out a business card and handed it to her. "He lost his wallet in Columbus. I'm trying to return it to him."

My business card had the usual effect on her, which is to say the look on her face matched the expression people get finding half a bug in their house Caesar salad.

"So why are you here?"

I explained about finding the receipt.

"I can ask my manager," she said doubtfully.

"Thank you. Also—?"

"Yes?"

"Could you warm up the pie?"

As she disappeared around the corner, my thoughts were interrupted by the sound of "Welcome to the Jungle" emitting from my back pocket. My heart sped up. The judge? I extracted the phone, and swallowed my disappointment when I saw it was Bonnie calling.

"That was fast."

"Sure, not counting the nap I just took. Anyway, that license? Gary Phipps from Missouri? He's not showing up anywhere, other than a Wikipedia page about retired motocross racers. It's probably fake."

"I should have figured. He just didn't have the ring of truth about him. Any connection to the realty company? Or the judge?"

"None that I could find."

"Anything on Rumford itself?"

"Not a whole lot. Looks like a medium-sized business, head-quarters in Hilliard." The fast-growing suburb on the northwest side of Columbus was a booming conglomeration of subdivisions, big box stores, and vanishing farmland. No wetlands to speak of. "They do a lot of small retail plazas. Not a huge player, as far as I can tell, but not small either."

"And that's what's planned for Mendon Woods?"

"Hard to say. They want commercial zoning, but there's nothing concrete beyond that. Pretty vague."

Carefully, I said, "And this judge. Laura Porter—the one overseeing that case. She's supposed to rule soon?"

"Relatively soon, yes."

"Meaning what?"

"She delayed things recently at the state's request. They wanted to do another survey on this bird."

"What bird?"

"Hang on." I heard the click-clacking of keys. "It's called a coastal tanager."

"Right." I remembered the marker at the park along the walkway. "What's the survey about?"

"To see how many are left. Apparently Mendon Woods is one of their last habitats in Ohio."

I recalled Deanna Fleischer's timely appearance at the pond as Tear Drop prepared to do his worst. Is that what she'd been up to—conducting a new count of coastal tanagers?

I said, "What did the survey show?"

"It hasn't come back yet. I guess she's still waiting for it. That guy's not happy about it, according to one article I read."

"Which guy?"

"One of the lawyers."

"For who—the realty company?" I imagined the delay would be maddening for a business; time is money and all that.

"No—for the environmentalists. He asked the judge what the problem was finishing the report. But the lawyer for the realty company had no objections. Told the judge they could take as long as they needed."

Our conversation was interrupted by my waitress returning with the dessert and a coffee refill. By my count a minute or two later than cutting a slice of pie, microwaving it, dishing on ice cream, and showing the photo around should have taken. But maybe it was my imagination. I apologized and told Bonnie I'd have to call her back.

The waitress deposited my pie in front of me and set the license on the table beside it. "Nobody's seen him."

"They're sure?"

"Yes," she said confidently. "Also, my manager said to tell you we don't want any trouble."

"That makes two of us. Thanks for your help, anyway. Oh—ma'am?"

Reluctantly she turned back.

"The man, on the flier. By the front door. The missing person."

"Todd? What about him?"

"Who is he?"

"What do you mean?"

"I mean, I guess, do you know him?"

"I know his family. It's a close community."

"Any idea what happened?"

A pause while her left hand rose to adjust a loose strand of hair. "He disappeared."

"From where? If I may ask?"

"From Heyder's Creek. He'd been over there fishing."

"It's a creek?"

"Actually, it's more of a swamp," she said.

14

SHE GAVE ME THE basics. Orick told his girlfriend he was going fishing one Sunday morning in June. Drove his pickup to an access point of a tributary feeding the swamp known as Heyder's Creek. He was only supposed to be a couple of hours, since he planned to take said girlfriend to Down Home Buffet for Sunday brunch for her birthday. But sometime after eleven in the morning he stopped returning her texts. By one o'clock the girlfriend's frustration at his absence turned to concern. She and her father and Orick's father went looking. They found his truck, but no sign of the young man. He hadn't been seen since.

"Any theories?"

"Plenty." She plucked at the lace fringe on the wrist of her sleeve. "Most of them ridiculous."

"Like what?"

"Serial killer, grabbed by some kind of mutant snake, faked his death."

"What do you think?"

"I have no idea. It's sad, I'll tell you that. He was a good kid." She paused again, looking toward the door. "Did you need anything else?"

"I guess not, thanks."

I took a drink of coffee and dug into the pie. Delicious, indeed, but not warmed, I noticed. I checked my messages while I ate, harboring another fantasy I might have heard from the judge. But the text screen was blank except for a reminder from my ex, Kym—Mike's mom—of his upcoming scrimmage. I thought back to Mike's and my parting on the ball field, the way I'd blown him off—again—because of work. The fact that mortal danger might be involved might make a difference for me, but not for him. I told Kym I'd be there. I texted Crystal to see if Joe would be available to tag along. In some ways the half brothers couldn't have been more different. Mike was an extrovert with few unvoiced opinions and a personality that hovered between engaging and abrasive—talk about a chip off the old block. Joe, by contrast, was the classic introvert, head always in a book and brow furrowed at whatever was going on inside his head, which was increasingly hard to get into. Maybe some of me there too. Somehow the two managed to get along, perhaps united by the experience of surviving my many misfires as a dad. The same allegiance shared by a band of brothers who've been to war together? I shook my head at the thought, finished my pie, and called Bonnie back.

"Sorry about that. There was one other thing. Could you check campaign finance records for the judge?"

"Sure. Anything in particular?"

"Not really. Maybe anyone connected with either side of the Mendon Woods case. The developer and the environmentalists."

"Can judges get contributions like that? For a case they're sitting on?"

"Anybody can contribute as long as they follow the rules. Just let me know what you find."

She told me she would. I thanked her and said I'd be in touch and at the last moment asked her how things had gone at the café and with Anne. She said fine. I thought about texting Anne to . . . what? Thank her for staying friends with Bonnie? Eating at what had once been a favorite restaurant of ours? Being a disgustingly nice person? I decided against it. Old wounds and all that. After a last swig of coffee, I took my check and walked to the front. The hostess scooted over to the cash register. I paid her, scooped a peppermint out of a bowl, and headed for the exit. I paused in front of the missing-person flier. Todd Orick stared back at me, a grin on his bearded face. Judging from the angle, the picture was likely a selfie, maybe pulled from Facebook. The coincidence wasn't lost on me—two swamps, two types of trouble—but could it be more than that? I would have said no, except for the Down Home Buffet receipt in my attacker's wallet. On a whim I pulled out my phone and took a picture of the flier.

I pocketed the phone, stepped outside and stopped, staring. Another coincidence? How else to explain the police cruiser parked behind my van, blocking my way out.

THE DECAL ON THE brown cruiser said Mohican Township Police Department. As I weighed my options, the driver's-side door opened and a uniformed woman hauled herself out of the vehicle.

"How's it going?" she said.

"Fine. Yourself?"

"Not too bad, thanks. You have a moment?"

"I suppose. Is this about the pie?"

"The pie?"

"They didn't warm it up like I asked. But I decided not to file a formal complaint after all."

She studied my face, trying to decide if I was teasing her or just being a jackass. In her defense, I'm capable of doing both at the same time. You should see what I can do with a stick of Wrigley's and a decent pair of sneakers.

"Is that so?"

"I mean, I figure extenuating circumstances and all."

"Oh yeah?"

"Well, I'm thinking my waitress got distracted while she was calling you. Hard to blame her, really."

"I'm sorry?"

"Not that it's important. I'd probably have done the same thing, in her shoes. Stranger in town and all—why not alert the authorities? Perfectly natural reaction. So, is there something I can do for you, Officer?"

She didn't respond. She had a funny look on her face as she studied mine. That puzzled me until I remembered mine still bore evidence of my run-in with Tear Drop. I studied her in return. Someplace in her forties, blonde-returning-to-black-roots hair pulled into a bun, green eyes set in a no-nonsense face absent any makeup. Ex-military bearing—I was guessing marines, but maybe army—with a solid figure to match. She looked about as good in department-issued trousers as female cops usually do. The name on the badge said G. Pugh. When she didn't respond, I repeated the question.

She said, "Bev mentioned you were looking for someone."

"Bev—that's my waitress?"

"That's right."

"Bev is correct, then."

"Mind if I ask who it is? This guy whose picture you showed?"

"Not at all. The more the merrier." I retrieved the driver's license of Gary Phipps from Springfield, Missouri. I explained it was probably fake. She took it, examined it, and without looking up said, "You're a private eye."

"Yes."

"From Columbus."

I conceded her point.

"You have a license?"

"Sure." I pulled that and a business card out of my wallet and handed them both over. Her appearance and interest in my investigation were intriguing. But I couldn't see the point of arguing with her yet, although I was drawing the line at providing my Kroger card.

She made a production of examining my PI credentials, then handed that and my license back. My business card went into a back pocket.

She said, "Andy Hayes, private eye." Statement, not a question. A look in her eyes I still couldn't read. Had she heard of me, and was making the fact known, or was she just yanking my chain? Or both? Maybe we were both good at multitasking.

"So, what's your interest in this guy?" She tapped Tear Drop's license.

"It depends. Have you seen him?"

"How about you answer my question first."

"My interest is that he and I had a disagreement this morning."

Eyes on and off my bruised face. "About what?"

"The details aren't important. But he had a receipt in his wallet for this place"—I pointed backwards with an outstretched thumb at the restaurant—"and I decided to see what I could find out."

"How'd you come by his wallet?"

"He dropped it during our chat."

"Long way from Columbus."

"It was a nice day for a drive."

"Sure it was."

"My turn. Do you know him?"

She shook her head.

"You're sure?"

"Yes. Why wouldn't I be?"

"I don't know, other than why speed on over so quickly? I show the guy's license to Bev and you're here ten minutes later. Seems fishy. Plus rude, since my pie didn't get warmed up."

"I think you should be careful what you say—"

"Here's what I think. I think this has something to do with Todd Orick."

The left side of her mouth twitched almost imperceptibly, as if she were trying to dislodge a fly without raising a hand. "And why would you say that?"

"Because me and that guy"—I pointed to the driver's license in her hand—"had a rather intense conversation in a swamp down in Columbus this morning. And that guy, Todd Orick, disappeared in a swamp up here, not far from a restaurant Mr. Not Gary Phipps from Springfield, Missouri, had a receipt for in his wallet. Could be a stretch, but since you asked: that's why I would say that."

As I spoke, I tried to decide whether to mention the judge. To bring up her own connection to swamps. I opted against it in the end, unsure of where I stood with Officer G. Pugh. Whose side she was on. In either case, she didn't respond right away. She looked at the fake license, looked at me, and looked past me to the entrance to Down Home Buffet. If I was furthering my guess about her past, I'd say ex–military police with a drawer full of stories about crap she'd taken as a woman with a badge in the armed forces but also a second drawer with commendations to show she didn't let it get to her—much.

"In town long, Mr. Hayes?"

"Call me Andy."

"Could you answer the question, please?"

"Well, it depends."

"On what?"

"On if I find that guy. And if I decide to come back here for dinner."

"Maybe that's not such a good idea."

"Really? The board in there said the special was sirloin tips on egg noodles. That's one of my favorites."

"I mean looking for that guy."

"Why not?"

"Just a bit of advice."

"Advice, or a warning?"

"Interpret it as you'd like."

"In that case, thank you, I think. Was there anything else?"

Officer G. Pugh took a last look at my face. As if she were trying to decide something for herself, something she wasn't quite certain of. To ramp up the hard-ass routine? Or answer my question against her better judgment.

"Have a nice day, Mr. Hayes."

"You too, Officer."

I watched as she retreated into her cruiser, backed up, swung wide, and drove off without even so much as a wave goodbye. I waved anyway. Then I climbed into my van, pulled out my phone, and set about tracking down the family of Todd Orick. Maybe I'd get more out of them than Officer Pugh.

15

DAVID AND FRANCINE ORICK Lived in a faded yellow ranch perched on the side of a small hill at the end of a winding gravel driveway five miles down the road from Down Home Buffet and two hundred yards below a forested ridge from a wind turbine. You saw more and more of them in Ohio every year, the updated equivalent of the solitary oil and gas rigs that dotted farm fields across the state. The equipment changed, but the relentless pursuit of energy continued.

On my arrival I knocked twice, setting off a barking dog inside but no one else. It was pushing four o'clock; still early if they worked. I was writing out a message when a pickup truck turned up the drive and approached. A heavyset couple in their mid- to late fifties emerged from the truck a moment later.

"Help you?" a man said, putting himself between me and the woman with him as he walked up. He was balding, with a mustache and thick-lensed eyeglasses.

I handed him my card and explained that I'd come across the case of Todd and was hoping to ask them some questions.

"About what?"

Without getting into specifics, I related the possible connection between Mendon Woods and Heyder's Creek.

"You think that place in Columbus has something to do with Todd?"

"I don't know. It's quite possible it doesn't. But somebody I met at the Columbus swamp had been at Down Home Buffet recently, which is where I heard about Todd. I figured as long as I was up here . . . "

The man exchanged glances with the woman. She too wore glasses and kept her brown-gray hair short. A small silver cross hung on a chain around her neck.

"You'd better come inside," the man said after a minute.

"HAVE YOU TALKED TO the police up here?" Mrs. Orick said. Though her name was Francine, everyone called her Fran. She was making coffee in the kitchen. I seated myself on a couch opposite her husband in the adjoining living room. The house was neat and well kept, carpeted wall to wall and heavy on light-blue upholstered furniture. Walls hung with family photos and a lone painting of a deer standing at the edge of a heavy wood. The dog, a nondescript mutt who ceased barking as soon as he saw the Oricks come inside, lay at Mr. Orick's feet. "Todd's dog," he said, with no further explanation.

I called out to Fran, "Just in passing. Officer Pugh? She's aware of my interest."

"She's been a godsend," Fran said. "I don't know what we would have done without her."

"I can imagine," I said, trying to reconcile that observation with the suspicion and flat affect and—no other way to put it—standoffish attitude I'd detected in the officer. "I'm sorry to trouble you, and I don't mean to raise any expectations about your son. I don't have any information about him, as it relates to what happened up here."

"You're a private detective?" Dave said.

"An investigator, yes."

"And there's an issue with the swamp down in Columbus?"

I explained about the lawsuit.

"Heyder's Creek is part of that?"

"Not that I'm aware of. But if it's not too much trouble, I'm interested in what happened to Todd. If by some chance there's a connection."

He didn't respond. I saw that he couldn't, as the pain of his missing son brightened his eyes.

"We wish we knew," Fran said, coming into the living room with mugs of coffee for her husband and me. She returned to the kitchen and retrieved her own cup. "He just vanished. They found his truck and a few weeks later, one of his wading boots. And that was it. It's like he disappeared into thin air."

"What do the police think happened?"

"It's just Gloria at this point." Reading the question on my face, she added: "Officer Pugh. She doesn't know either. The suspicion is he drowned, but that don't make much sense. He was a good swimmer, wasn't he, Dave?"

"Yes," her husband said.

"We'd just like some closure," Fran said. "It would make it all a little easier."

I nodded, though in truth I couldn't imagine how anything would make the loss of their son bearable. I thought about my own boys and what I'd feel like in similar circumstances. I thought regretfully of Mike's and my conversation on the ball field. Thought of Joe, at his Thurber House writing camp this week, how vulnerable he could be emotionally.

"Do you have any pictures of Todd? Other than the one—"

"The one on the flier?" Fran said. She nodded. "I've got a few on my iPad."

She retrieved the tablet from a back room and opened up the photo roll. She showed me a series of pictures, variations of the same shot: a young man with a smile halfway between mischievous and engaging. The kind of kid who in high school would have been familiar with detention but not suspension. A few pictures showed him goofing off with a round girl with a pretty face—his girlfriend, his mother confirmed.

"Is that him in the swamp?" I examined a picture of him grinning at the camera, brackish water behind him, a tree branch jutting out in the near distance.

"He took that a week before he disappeared," his mother said, her voice catching. "He made that his profile picture."

I asked as gently as possible if she would be able to send the photo to me, and gave her my cell phone number.

"I won't keep you any longer. You've been more than generous with your time. If I come across anything involving Todd, I'll be sure to let you know."

"Do you think there's anything else?" Fran said.

"I don't know. I'm sure the police—I'm sure Gloria is being diligent. But if there is—"

"Not diligent enough," Dave said.

"What do you mean?"

"Dave," Fran said.

"Diligent is finding him," he continued. "Dead or alive. And that ain't happened yet. And probably never will, from the looks of it."

16

DAVE WALKED ME OUTSIDE, The dog following. Approaching my van, I glanced up at the turbine.

"Bother you, that thing being so close?"

He looked up. "Not really. You hardly hear it. Still wish to hell they'd get rid of it."

"Why?"

"Dangerous, that's why."

"Dangerous? How—"

"Plus it's a piss-poor investment up here. People come to Mohican County to look at leaves and camp and ski and fish. That thing's ruining the views. And they're talking about more, if something don't stop it."

I nodded. I'd heard similar objections to wind turbines before. I wondered what he meant by dangerous but decided against inquiring. I'd already intruded enough into his life. Instead, I asked him for directions to the swamp and the lane where Todd's truck was found. The look on his face as he told me made me wish I'd just Googled it instead.

"Thanks again."

He nodded, turned, and trudged back inside, not waiting for me to leave.

It took me fifteen minutes driving in the opposite direction to find Heyder's Creek, but soon enough I was pulling my van onto a rutted mud lane bisecting a field of overgrown grass and ripening goldenrod and Queen Anne's lace, doing my best not to strand myself. A cornfield filled several acres of ground behind me, with a stand of woods on my right, the trees a mass of green in the humid August air. I saw a few tree trunks as wide as columns fronting an old-fashioned bank, indicating the forest could be at least a hundred years old, if not more. Virgin timber was rare in Ohio, which was all but deforested by the end of the nineteenth century, but here and there individual patches survived the axe.

Inside the forest, under the canopy of trees, it was shadier but not much cooler, and the air was filled with bugs. Also absent any sound of the outer world—a far cry from the more urbanized feel of Mendon Woods. The path I followed was overgrown with smaller plants. I recalled the old poison ivy warning—leaves of three, let it be, leaves of five, let it thrive. But which was which? I caught a couple of snatches of birdsong overhead, including the lone notes of one I recognized, that of a cardinal, thanks to incessant nagging by my dad, who prided himself on knowing that kind of thing. But as for the others, I couldn't tell a tufted titmouse from a blue jay—or a coastal tanager.

After ten minutes of walking, the trees thinned and I saw standing water ahead. After another minute I stood in front of a large pond. I retrieved my phone and examined the photo Mrs. Orick sent me. I was in almost the same place Todd stood when he snapped the picture. I realized now, staring at it, that there was a bird on the branch behind him—I looked around and found the same branch. It was empty today. Todd had gotten a lucky shot. I turned back to the pond. Just as in Mendon Woods, cattails and reeds ringed the far end. Blue-and-green dragonflies skimmed the water's surface like winged jewels. Off to my left, a tall gray heron hunted its own frogs in a bed of lilies, unaware or uncaring of my presence, gingerly raising and lowering its legs like an old man hunting his morning paper in a flowerbed. The cousin of the bird I'd seen that morning in Columbus? I heard a cry and looked up and saw a hawk circling overhead. I'd hardly call myself a nature guy. I'm more content these days to spend time reading in my backyard or kibitzing with the two Kevins at Schiller Park. Kevin M. played trombone in the Ohio State marching band, so we occasionally chat about our shared experiences in Ohio Stadium—his with a happier outcome than mine. But as someone who grew up in the pre-internet age and spent a fair share of time outdoors as a kid, I could appreciate what coming here must have meant to Todd Orick.

A commotion, off to my left. The heron had struck. I watched as it lifted its beak and gulped down a water creature of one kind or another. Crayfish? Bluegill? I thought of the old workplace-bulletin-board cartoon of a frog halfway down a bird's gullet, grasping the bird's throat to save itself. *"Never give up,"* the caption went. Not for this heron's prey, apparently.

I walked left, following a deer trail around the pond. I tread quietly, and looked side to side and behind me often, wary of a repeat of this morning's encounter. Whoever Tear Drop was, he would have had plenty of time to drive here after rushing away from Mendon Woods. And he'd followed me once, after all. The hike around the water took twenty minutes. Finished, I snapped a few pictures with my phone, including one trying to replicate the selfie Todd made that ended up as his Facebook profile photo, without the bird on the branch.

The day had gotten away from me, and shadows were starting to fall across the field as I emerged from the forest and left the swamp behind. I looked at the wind turbine on the far ridge, tiny in perspective from here, and then dropped my eyes to an abandoned barn I hadn't seen before on the opposite side of the cornfield. I looked closer; a smudge of dust was rising from the side. Just for a second I caught a glimpse of metal as a car drove in and then out of my peripheral vision. It might have been my imagination, but the color looked a lot like the brown of the Mohican Township police cruiser that Officer Pugh parked behind my van back at Down Home Buffet. What was in that barn, I wondered. I turned around. And what—or whose body?—was in that swamp?

17

BACK IN MY VAN I made a spur-of-the moment decision. I texted Kevin M. and confirmed I wouldn't be back tonight and asked if he could let the dog out and feed the cat. He responded in the form of a short video of Hopalong at Schiller Park with the pugs. Running back and forth, rolling around on the grass, my Lab looked like a different dog, younger and friskier than I'd seen him in years. Guiltily, I thought of his solitary existence when I was around. The long days when I was hunting straying spouses. The longer nights when I earned extra cash pulling security shifts at Nationwide Arena. He was well fed, warm in the winter and cool in the summer, and got a walk most days. But like a lot of creatures in my life—I thought briefly again of Anne—he probably deserved better.

I looked up lodging options on my phone. A few minutes later I was at a Motel 6 off Route 13, arranging to stay the night. Something told me there was more to do up here. I had no idea if the judge was in the area. But thanks to her absent Lexus, I didn't think she was in Columbus, and I knew she was in trouble. And the trouble had something to do with a swamp and a guy with a tear drop on his cheek. And now there was a second swamp, and a missing person. Related? Who knew? I thought idly of the abandoned barn by Heyder's Creek. That might bear further investigation. I considered the Oricks, the pain in their eyes. It might be worth asking around a little more, find other people who knew Todd. Maybe they could shed light on what happened to him. Maybe I could find something Officer Pugh missed.

Mohican Township was the first burg inside Mohican County, a mostly rural community filled with a lot of farms, a lot of Amish, and a lot of timber. The county seat was fifteen miles in the opposite direction, compared to a five-minute drive into Mansfield, the biggest city nearby. I opted for the latter. I put my investigating skills to work and ended up at the Phoenix, a brew pub in an old converted mortuary in a renovated corner of downtown in the shadow of tall, abandoned industrial buildings that once employed thousands. The story of almost every small city in Ohio, as I'd been reading in *Glass House*. I brought the book with me inside, ordered a house IPA, and called a pizza shop around the corner that delivered. I read a chapter, then set the book on the table beside my phone to have a look around. I picked up my phone almost immediately as a number I didn't recognize lit up the screen.

"It's Officer Pugh. From the restaurant?"

"I recall our meeting with pleasure—"

"You went to the Oricks' house."

I confirmed the accuracy of the information.

"Why did you do that?"

"I wanted to ask them questions about their son. To see if anything they said might connect to what happened at Mendon Woods."

"Where?"

I reminded her of the swamp in Columbus.

"They're upset."

"I'm sorry to hear that. I take it they called you?"

"You showing up like that took them aback. They want to know if there's something going on. A break in the case or something. They said you weren't very forthcoming."

"I tried to be upfront. Make it clear I was looking at something on the periphery of what might have happened to Todd. I wasn't a jerk about it, I promise. Dave invited me in, for what it's worth."

"Not much. What was he supposed to do? I would have appreciated a heads-up that you were going out there. I could have come along, helped explain to the Oricks what was happening. Made it easier for them. Plus, this is still my case."

"I understand that. But it didn't occur to me to ask your permission to conduct my own investigation. Unless that's how things operate up here."

"How things operate up here is none of your business. Where are you?"

"I'm sorry?"

"Are you back in Columbus?"

"And that would be none of your—"

"Listen, Hayes—"

"But in the interest of goodwill, I'm happy to let you know I'm still up here, just for a day or so."

"Why?"

"I need to satisfy myself on a couple points."

"Like what?" she said.

"Like a couple of points."

"Long way to come based on a receipt in a wallet."

"I'm very thorough."

"I'm aware of that."

"You are?"

"Do me a favor, all right?"

"If I can."

"I can't stop you from poking around. But maybe at least think about the impact you're having? You saw Todd's parents, how they are. They're not alone, starting with his girlfriend, who's devastated. No matter what happened to him, people are in pain."

"I understand."

"Do you?"

"I just said I did."

A woman appeared at my table with a box of pizza. I nodded and told Pugh I had to go. She asked me where I was staying. I said it had been good speaking with her. I promised I'd be sensitive with my inquiries. I hung up, took the pizza, handed the woman a twenty, and signaled for another beer.

A third IPA later, with most of the pizza gone, I thought about driving back to the swamp and checking out the barn. But I realized with night fallen I wasn't exactly sure how to return there. It had also been a long day, with a rigorous conversation at Mendon Woods starting to settle in at the back of my eyes in the form of a headache that wasn't going away anytime soon. I drove back to the motel instead. I parked and opened the back of the van and retrieved the go bag I keep there for emergency high-level security operations and for cloudbursts at the dog park. I went inside and sat on the bed. I regretted leaving my laptop in Columbus; it would have made researching leads easier. Instead, I pretended to look up more information about the judge and Todd Orick and Mendon Woods and Heyder's Creek on my phone. Ten minutes later I was asleep.

I slept longer than intended, waking around eight o'clock the next morning. I realized I was having trouble swallowing thanks to Tear Drop's handiwork. I shaved carefully, showered and changed clothes. I checked my messages. After thinking things over, I decided the best thing was to learn everything I could about Todd Orick, and see if anything connected him with Mendon Woods. Maybe find his girlfriend. But first I needed breakfast. I left the room, walked down the hall, nodded at the clerk reading the *Mansfield News-Journal* at the counter, and walked outside. And stared at my van for the second time in two days.

All four tires were slashed on my Odyssey, which had sunk to the rims like an aging elephant unable to right itself.

18

"I'VE GOT A LITTLE problem."

"So do I," Officer Pugh said. "Do you know what time it is?"

"As a matter of fact I do. Which is somewhat related to my problem."

Over the phone, I explained the situation with my van. I wasn't exactly sure why I decided to call her. But the probing nature of our conversation the night before while I sat at the Phoenix nursing my IPA had my suspicions aroused.

I said, "I can always call the Mohican County sheriff's office. The clerk inside said that's this jurisdiction. Have a deputy—"

"Don't do that."

"Why not?"

"Just don't. Can you give me twenty minutes?"

"I suppose. Can you recommend a garage?"

She told me to call a place called Kirkwood's. I did, and they said they'd send a tow truck. While I waited I went back inside the motel and helped myself to a Styrofoam cup of coffee from the half-filled pot in the lobby. It looked and tasted as if it had been brewed the night before, around the time I checked in. Or maybe the night before that. I scrolled my phone in vain for messages from the judge while I waited.

Kirkwood's beat Officer Pugh by five minutes. The tow-truck operator was using chains and a hydraulic motor to haul the Odyssey onto a flatbed truck when the officer arrived. She greeted him by name and asked him to hold for a second. She took pictures of each tire.

When she finished, she said, "Have you had breakfast yet?"

"I've had coffee your friend there might be able to use for an oil change. Other than that, no."

"Me neither. C'mon. I'll give you a ride."

"IN TOWN LESS THAN twenty-four hours and already made some friends," Pugh said. "You work fast."

"I'm thinking it's time for the kids to get back to school. If they're bored enough to go around slashing tires on an out-of-town van with a big butt—"

"I don't think we're talking kids, Hayes."

We were back at Down Home Buffet, seated at a table with a view of the parking lot, including Pugh's cruiser. The hostess, a different high school–aged girl, far sleepier than her compatriot the day before, brought us directly to the table by the window, making me think Pugh was not a stranger here. My friend Bev was back on duty. She brought us both coffee without being asked. She skedaddled away just as efficiently before I could inquire if it was she or her manager who outed me to the cops. I guess it didn't matter at this point. It was just us and a few others in the dining room; the rush of early morning truckers past, the parade of coffee-klatsching seniors yet to come. I glanced around and settled my eyes on the Greenville Treaty painting.

I said, "Why do you say that?"

Pugh's turn to glance around.

"Couple reasons. First, I can't recall a report of slashed tires around here in a while. We're not a bunch of innocent hicks, OK? But our kids still gravitate toward TP-ing houses and Saran-wrapping cars for their shits and giggles."

"Believe it or not, we have houses covered in Charmin in Columbus too. Any other reason?"

She looked out the window at her cruiser. Beyond it the low central Ohio hills ran north, dark with trees.

"There's something funny going on with Heyder's Creek."

"That's the other reason you think it wasn't kids?"

She nodded.

"Funny like what?"

"Funny like, starting with Todd Orick."

"The fact he's missing—"

"He's not missing, Hayes."

"I thought—"

"I mean, yeah, he's missing. But he's dead. I'm sure of it."

BEV RETURNED AND TOOK our orders. I asked for pancakes and bacon and two eggs over easy. Pugh went for oatmeal and a fruit bowl. Both of us said more coffee would be great.

"How can you be sure he's dead?" I asked when Bev was gone.

"What other explanation is there? He's a bit of a screw-up, but nothing major. He was fishing without a license that day, but big deal. He has—*had*—a civilian job at the National Guard base in Mansfield. Not a good one, but a job. And a girlfriend willing to put up with his crap, which is saying something with Todd. I just can't see him running. He's either still in that swamp and he's muskrat food by now, or he's someplace else, but not far. And still dead."

"So when you said you hadn't seen the guy on the license I showed around—"

"I was telling the truth. I haven't seen that particular guy, that I know of. But—"

"But what?"

"But like I said, something funny's going on. And I think Todd is related to it. And now you. And your tires."

"Me?"

"Who did you tell you were staying at that Motel 6?"

"No one."

"You sure?"

"Positive. Not even my dog sitters."

"And yet your tires, out of everyone else's in that parking lot, are the ones that get cut?"

I told her I saw her point.

"But how's that related to Heyder's Creek?"

"Somebody's interested in that place," she said. "Somebody who pays attention when strangers come to town."

"Like who?"

"Like maybe people who do things to kids in swamps."

19

I TOOK A DRINK of coffee. It was ambrosia compared to the stuff from the Motel 6 lobby. Or nectar—I can never keep those straight.

I said, "You also pay attention when strangers come to town."

"Of course I do. It's my job."

"Were you in the military?"

Eyes narrowed. "Yes."

"Which branch?"

"Army."

"MP?"

"How did you know that?"

"I pay attention to people who pay attention to strangers in town. So what kind of interest are we talking? With the swamp, I mean?"

"You see people down there from time to time."

"People like who?"

"People who don't look like they belong in swamps. People without fishing poles or traps or shotguns in hunting season."

"People like they're from Springfield, Missouri?" I reminded her of the fake name and address on Tear Drop's driver's license.

"Who knows who they are? That's the whole point."

"Which is why—"

"Which is one of the reasons I came over when I, you know, heard you were here."

"Heard?"

The side of her mouth twitched again, and her face hardened. "OK—got tipped. It's a small community, Hayes. We look out for each other. 'See something, say something' isn't just for you big-city boys." She paused. "You should know that better than most."

"Why do you say that?"

"Forget it. The thing is, at first I thought maybe you were connected to whoever is poking around down there. By Heyder's Creek."

"I'm not, just for the record."

"I believe you."

"Good to hear—"

"But after what happened, it still seemed odd when you showed up."

"You mean what happened with Todd?"

She shook her head. "After that. I was down at the swamp a few weeks ago, early evening. After Todd disappeared. I go from time to time to search, since there doesn't seem to be anything else to do at this point. I was parked by the cornfield, figuring out my approach, when a car pulled in behind me. I was around a bend, so he wouldn't have seen me until he made the same turn. He took off in a hurry, I can tell you that."

"Who was it?"

"I don't know. But I managed to turn around and snap a picture and got the plate. Came back to a rental. After a couple calls I traced it to something called PG Inc."

"Procter & Gamble?" The consumer goods behemoth was headquartered in Cincinnati, which would make sense.

Gloria shook her head. "The address is a P.O. box registered out of Delaware, so good luck finding out anything about it. At least I couldn't. But just for the heck of it, the next day I go into town and try looking it up at the Recorder's Office. See if some-body's pulled permits for that land or if there's a sale pending or something. Anything that might explain the people I've seen down there."

"Did it?"

She shook her head. "And then the next day, another odd thing happened."

"Odd how?"

"Out of the blue, my chief calls me into his office."

"For what?"

"He wanted to know what I'd been up to, looking at that stuff. I was honest with him, told him it was nothing more than following a loose thread, trying to see if I could find out anything that might shed light on what happened to Todd. I made it clear I didn't have anything solid to go on. Just the opposite—said I was probably grasping at straws."

I thought about something. "How'd he know you were looking that company up?"

A small smile. "Score one for the private dick. A good question. Somebody in the recorder's office dropped a dime, apparently."

"So what happened?"

"My chief told me in no uncertain terms to drop what I was doing. That I had more important things to focus on. We've got the same shit up here as you do in Columbus, these days—opioids, shootings, trafficking. He told me to concentrate on that. I pushed back a little, asked him why. I could tell he was getting uncomfortable. But he wouldn't back down until I agreed."

"Any idea where that was coming from?"

"That day, no. But the next day I find a note in my mailbox. From Sandy, the department secretary. Told me to meet her here for lunch. Not unusual, since we both stop in a lot. When I got here, she chatted about a bunch of stuff, until we had our food. Then she told me something really interesting."

I leaned forward, intent on the story.

"She said the Mohican County sheriff called the chief the afternoon before. I matched the times up and realized the call came within fifteen minutes of my showing up in the recorder's office."

"Did she say why he was calling?"

"She didn't know. But it's not really hard to figure out, is it?"

I let the implication sink in before replying. "You're saying the fix is in."

"It sure seems that way. For some reason they don't want me digging into PG Inc. and whatever or whoever is interested in Heyder's Creek."

"So that's—"

"That's why I was so suspicious of you at first. If I couldn't trust the sheriff, what was I supposed to think about a private eye from Columbus snooping around?"

"You think the powers that be here know what happened to Todd? And they're covering it up for some reason? That's a scary accusation."

"I know it is. I also have no idea if it's true. It sounds far-fetched, when I hear it out loud like that. And maybe I should have dropped it then. Because the chief's right about the problems we got going on around here—hell, a state trooper just busted a guy with five kilos of heroin in his pickup truck two weeks ago."

"But?"

"There's an abandoned farm on the other side of a cornfield from Heyder's Creek. Couple got foreclosed on back in 2008, and it's been sitting fallow ever since."

"Yeah. I saw it."

"You did?"

I explained about my exploration of the swamp after talking to Todd Orick's parents. How much it reminded me of Mendon Woods, without guys pulling knives on me.

"Knives?"

"Let's just say my conversation in the swamp in Columbus was particularly intense."

"Good to know, with everything going on."

"Why's that?"

Gloria said, "Two weeks ago somebody passing at night called to report lights in that barn. I'm thinking kids or something. I go down but nobody's around and everything's locked up tight. Later, though, with everything happening, I wondered. I asked the chief about taking a look, getting a warrant tied to Todd's disappearance."

"Let me guess."

"No go. Focus on the problems at hand. We're spread too thin as it is."

"Which—if I may? Sounds like you sort of are, right? You can't be a big department."

She bristled, and her eyes darkened. "Listen—"

"Relax, would you? It wasn't a criticism. I know what it's like in cop shops these days. Hell, they're stretched in Columbus, and that's the state capital. I'm just wondering if maybe it's a reality that your chief's using to his advantage."

The corner of her mouth twitched and her face softened a bit. "You may be right. Which I guess has me thinking."

"About what?"

"That there might be answers to what happened to Todd inside that barn."

20

LETTING HER WORDS SINK in, I glanced again at the painting of the Treaty of Greenville. It's probably my imagination, but every time I see it, I find myself looking at the face of the Indian in the painting's left-hand corner, a warrior examining the goings-on, and imagine him saying, "Well, fuck. Sold down the river again."

I said, "Why not just go into the barn yourself? On the pretense of chasing kids or, I don't know, checking on a wounded owl or something? Weren't you there yesterday?"

"How did you—"

"I saw your car as I was leaving."

"Yeah, that was me. Well, the reason I can't go in is our owls are too tough. They hardly ever need help."

"You know what I mean—"

"Of course I do. I'm tempted, believe me. Because I don't like being told no. But if whatever's going on reaches into the sheriff's office? I need to be very, very careful. I got a ways to go before my pension kicks in."

"Smart. But here's the thing. I don't have a pension."

"So?"

"So, unlike you, I also don't need a warrant. And I have no idea if the owls up here are tough or not. I'm thinking that I arranged for someone to look after my dog. And a cat, but that's another story. So I'm a free man, with the day before me."

Bev appeared again, freshened our coffee, shot a knowing look at Officer Pugh, and scurried off.

Gloria said, "I can't condone you breaking the law."

"I'm not asking you to. I'm not telling you anything. I'm just talking out loud, being chatty. Probably all this coffee Bev keeps serving us."

"Chatty, huh? Nothing to do with your friend with the knife and the intense conversation you had?"

"What can I tell you? I'm a curious guy, especially when other guys come at me with blades—"

"That's obvious. But it makes me wonder if I'm getting the entire story."

"What do you mean?"

"Well, normally I wouldn't mind a couple of half-truths, since that's most of what I deal with all day long. But with everything else going on right now? Forgive me if I'm skeptical."

"You're forgiven."

"Anything you want to add to your statement?"

"Maybe."

"I'm all ears."

I stalled by drinking more coffee. "The thing is, Officer—"

"It's Gloria, OK? 'Officer' is for if and when I put cuffs on you."

"That's good to know. Then I'm Andy—"

"I know who you are, Hayes. You were saying?"

I hesitated. I didn't doubt for a second that Pugh—that Gloria—would take me down and slap cuffs on my hands and read me my rights, and not in her indoor voice, if our relationship turned sour. But I also recognized that she'd gone out on a limb by telling me about the possible collusion of higher-ups in relation to a man's mysterious disappearance. Way out, come to think of it, which had me speculating about her own motives. I was guessing it wasn't my winning personality, or the attraction of a van with a big butt. What then?

I went out on my own limb and gave her the G-rated version of my concerns about the judge, and why it was hard for me to dismiss Laura's cryptic clue about Mendon Woods given the subsequent attack and now an apparent connection, however tenuous, with a missing person and another swamp.

"A kidnapped judge? Who's running for the Ohio Supreme Court? That's some serious shit."

"Whoa—I don't know if she's been kidnapped." I reminded her about the call in the conference room in the sheriff's office. The impression that Laura was both unharmed but also not free to move safely around the cabin. "But I owe it to her to find out what's really going on."

"Why?"

"What?"

"Why do you owe it to her? You were a part-time bodyguard for a couple of weeks, right?"

"She's a paying client." I recalled the dollar bill I coaxed out of the judge in her Lexus. "It's a professional responsibility."

"If you say so." But the look on her face said, not surprisingly, she wasn't buying it.

She said, "So what now?"

"Well, I guess I'll ask nicely if you could drop me by Kirkwood's. Once my van's ready I'm going to do some shopping. And then poke around a little more—carefully," I said, seeing her reaction. "And then wait for dark. Which reminds me. What time are you off duty?"

Eyes narrowing again. "Why?"

"I may need help finding that barn, especially at night. I get turned around easily."

21

BEV ARRIVED WITH OUR food. We dug in. I was hungrier than I thought. I told Gloria a little more about what I had in mind. She said she'd have to think about her role. I told her that was fine.

When we finished I followed her to the front of the restaurant and paid for both of us. I took two red-striped peppermints from the cut-glass bowl by the register and handed one to Gloria. I let her go first through the little entryway. She held open the glass door for a couple of ladies with hair the color of freshly rinsed cotton balls. We climbed into her cruiser. On the road running past the restaurant a tractor-trailer throttled down as it slowed to turn into Down Home Buffet's truckers lot. Beyond that a line of cars waited to turn onto the I-71 entrance ramp headed north.

Gloria checked the onboard laptop that police cruisers all come with nowadays, pulled out, and drove down the road for a minute without saying anything. We stopped for a red light and she turned to look at me.

"Listen, Hayes. I have to tell you something." Her voice formal again, the tone she might use standing by a car in the dark asking to see a license.

"OK."

"I know who you are."

"I'm sorry?"

"Andy Hayes. Private eye."

"I thought we established that."

"That's not what I mean."

"What, then?" She had that funny look on her face again. I couldn't tell if she was going to punch me or cry. Or both, and frankly she wouldn't be the first woman to respond to me that way.

"My daughter lives up here, but my son and his girlfriend are down in Columbus. I'd rather they were closer, but they went where the jobs are."

I nodded, not sure what to say. The light changed and she pulled across the intersection.

"Last summer they went downtown. To see fireworks. Them and some friends. They were just a block from Broad and High at ten, when they went off."

I didn't respond. There was no need. I understood where this was going. I stared out the front window as we drove past ripening soybean fields. Ahead was a sign for Snow Trails ski resort. I recalled a disastrous day of skiing with Mike and Joe there one winter, another daddy field trip gone awry.

"I just want to say—"

"Listen, Gloria . . ."

"Shut up for a second, would you?"

I shut up.

Red, White & Boom was one of the biggest fireworks displays in the Midwest. It was a highlight of Columbus's annual festival calendar. It pulled four hundred thousand people downtown, and that wasn't even counting the guys with red bandanas around their foreheads selling ice-cold bottles of water out of Coleman coolers at every other street corner. The previous year a white supremacist with visions of glory and access to a hell of a lot of ammonia nitrate attempted to turn a good number of those visitors into a giant cloud of particulate matter. Through a combination of stubbornness, a modicum of physical fitness, and pure luck, I squelched the plan at the last second. A lot of people got hurt anyway, but from bruises and ankle sprains incurred during a stampede rather than an eviscerating explosion.

Gloria tried again. "I just want to say—"

"Are they all right?"

"Who?"

"Your son and his girlfriend."

"They're fine. It's just that, when I heard your name—when Bev called. It brought back . . . "

"I'm glad they're OK."

She stared at me, hardness in her eyes, the set to her face the "Don't fuck with me" of the cop by the side of the road while the driver makes up an excuse for hitting eighty in the fifty zone the officer has already heard twice that day.

"I just wanted to say thanks. And that I'm off at eight. You're right about the roads out here. Rural Ohio. It's easy to get turned around."

22

THE COFFEE AT KIRKWOOD'S was only marginally better than the stuff at Motel 6, but I was pretty sure it had been made within the same lunar cycle. I poured myself a cup and sat down in the waiting room and picked up a two-year-old copy of *Field and Stream* and set it back down. I retrieved my phone and glanced at the background photo, a selfie I'd taken of Joe and Mike and me at a Columbus Crew game the previous fall. Since they were half brothers, and our respective relationships were each subject to separate custody agreements, it took some doing to get the three of us one in place. As a result, I treasured such visits—even bungled ski trips—although I was often at pains not to make a big show of it for fear of ruining the moment.

I checked my messages, suppressing the irrational hope I might have something from Laura. I needn't have bothered. Radio silence continued. I had an update e-mail from Bonnie, though nothing on the campaign donations. Instead, she'd sent me an online article from that day's *Columbus Dispatch*. The woman who had threatened Laura after her son's lengthy sentencing had been sentenced herself for contempt of court. Ninety days suspended sentence, a $300 fine, and forty hours of community service. And a warning from the judge—a different judge—to contain her emotions and remember that we're a nation based on the rule of law and respect for government institutions. It was clear from the look in the woman's eyes in the photo accompanying the article that the judge's lecture made about the same impression as a tsetse fly alighting on a bull rhino's haunch. But at least she didn't lash out again. Laura's name was mentioned, along with the old nickname—the Velvet Fist—but the article noted she wasn't present at sentencing. Nothing out of the ordinary—she didn't need to be there.

Couldn't be there, I thought.

"Mr. Hayes?"

I looked up. The Kirkwood's tow-truck guy.

"Yeah?"

"You're all set."

My wallet lighter by the equivalent of three car payments, I left the garage ten minutes later consoling myself by imagining my ride felt better thanks to a new set of tires. I checked my watch. Nearly eleven o'clock. I had three stops to make, and they might take some time.

Four, if you counted lunch.

First, I took Route 13 into town and fifteen minutes later walked into a Walmart. I greeted the greeter, took my bearings, regretted not bringing a compass, and set forth on my expedition.

Forty-five minutes later I emerged relatively unscathed with bags containing a dark black hoodie, black tracksuit pants, black sneakers, and a black fanny pack. I was ready for night maneuvers or an art gallery opening, whichever came first. I placed everything in the trunk of my van and headed back to Mansfield.

My second stop was the Mansfield–Richland County library on West Third. I signed up for a computer station, browsed the biography shelves until my turn arrived, sat down and logged onto the *News-Journal*'s website. I found and printed off every article available about the disappearance of Todd Orick. I wasn't sure what I was looking for, but I felt better once I retrieved the pile and started reading. In one, Todd's girlfriend made a tearful plea for his recovery. In another, his parents thanked a local birding group for conducting a search. In a third, the National Guard base where Todd worked pledged $1,000 for anyone with information leading to his safe return. Almost every story quoted Gloria.

Finished, I gathered up the articles, left the library, drove around the corner, and parked outside the Coney Island Diner. I went inside, assured myself no one I'd met in any swamps recently was keeping an eye on me, and ordered lunch. I ate at the counter while I read two chapters of *Glass House*. When I was done I walked down the street to Main Street Books and browsed for a couple minutes. Making up my mind, I bought a copy of *Wicked Women of Ohio*, figuring I'd better check to see if I ever dated any of them. I returned to my van, left town, and drove back into the country.

I followed the directions on my phone to Heyder's Creek. Instead of parking and hiking in, I took the country road around to the right and past the barn. I slowed to a stop to examine it. It sat a few hundred feet off the road, one of those old-style Ohio barns spacious enough to hold a township's worth of straw bales and solid enough to withstand a nuclear strike. It sported a fading Ohio Bicentennial mural on the wall facing the road, the design now pushing two decades old. The building was more gray than red. It looked abandoned, no doubt, but not utterly dilapidated. The farmhouse across the drive appeared in far worse shape, its shutters hanging at odd angles, porch sagging and windows boarded up. Was someone maintaining the one and not the other? I took some pictures without leaving my van, figuring out best approaches for my upcoming reconnaissance mission. Through the cornfield, I was thinking. I checked my watch. Midafternoon. Still a few hours to kill. I was deciding on my next move—more research, more preparation, more Coney Island dogs—when my phone rang. Bonnie.

"Hey," she said. "I think I found something interesting."

23

I KEPT MY EYE on the barn, trying to decide the best way inside. "Interesting like what?"

"Something I saw when I looked at the campaign finance records for that judge. I sent you that article, by the way."

"I saw that, thanks. You all right? You sound tired."

"No duh. I'm eating for three now, remember?"

"Time for more soul food?"

"Maybe. All this red meat is driving Troy a little crazy, since he's trying to go vegan. But he's being a good guy about it."

"No surprise there." Bonnie's boyfriend was devoted to her, as anyone spending even a few minutes with them would see.

"You still need to take him for that beer."

"For sure, once this is all over. So—campaign finance records. Interesting how?"

"For starters, I found a couple people from Rumford Realty who donated."

"How much?"

"Not a lot. Two hundred and fifty dollars each. As far as I can tell, one's from the president of the company and one's from his wife."

"What are their names?"

"Mr. and Mrs. Rumford, believe it or not. That's not the interesting thing, though."

"Oh?"

"I did a couple category sorts of the donations for the heck of it, to check for any patterns on addresses or anything else."

"And?"

"So the address for Rumford Realty is Britton Parkway on the west side. It's an industrial park, from the looks of it on Google Maps."

I told her I knew where it was.

"It turns out there were some bigger donations from a different company. But here's the funny thing. They came from the same address as Rumford."

"But not from people at Rumford?"

"Not as far as I can see. It's got another name. PG Inc."

"Say that again?"

She repeated the name.

I thought back to my conversation at the restaurant this morning with Gloria. The rental car she traced. PG Inc. Now that was interesting. I made the connection for Bonnie. I heard keys clacking in the background.

"Anything?" I said.

"Maybe. It shows up in a couple searches connected to cloud computing."

"Cloud computing?"

"Online information storage. Where all your songs on iTunes hang out when you're not listening to them."

"They're going to be pretty lonely on my cloud."

"You know what I mean. It's a little hard to tell what this company does—its website is kinda vague."

"Any swamps on there?"

"Swamps?"

"Never mind. So it's one of these storage companies?"

"Looks like. It's all the rage now. Amazon and Google and Facebook—they all need huge server farms to store all the information they generate. Especially with the AI stuff."

"What do you mean?"

"You know. Siri and all that. Artificial intelligence. It's the next wave of information storage. You need someplace to put the chips that let you talk to your toaster."

"As long as it doesn't get mouthy. Someplace like where?"

"Someplace big."

I thought about the acreage that constituted Mendon Woods. Except for the swamp, most of it was prime development land of the sort that got gobbled up all the time. Come to think of it, it was some of the last major space around Columbus that hadn't been slated for construction. Both Amazon and Facebook had opened that very type of information warehouse in and around the city in recent years to great acclaim from various mayors, state lawmakers, and the governor, all of whom were drooling to cash in on the information economy as soon as possible. It was part of Columbus's booming high-tech economy that was continuing to propel its growth. *Hey, Siri. Come to Ohio!*

I said, "These PG Inc. donations. How big?"

"Pretty sizable. Twelve thousand five hundred. I think that's the maximum. Looks like six of them from individual employees."

I did the math. Obviously timed for Laura's run for the Supreme Court. But also when the Mendon Woods lawsuit was on her docket.

"One-time donations?"

"All but one. Same-size donation from one guy earlier this year. I guess before the primary."

"Same address?"

"I don't think so. Someplace in Cleveland."

"Who is it?"

"Schiff somebody."

"OK." The name didn't mean anything. I asked her to e-mail me the names of all the contributors. "Thanks a lot," I added. "Be sure to send me an invoice. Maybe I'll throw in a couple of hamburgers."

"A couple?"

"One per baby?"

"At the rate I'm going, a cow apiece is more like it."

"I'm sure Troy will appreciate that."

"He's for anything that makes me happy. And less grouchy. You'll text him about the beer?"

"It's what I do best."

24

GLORIA LOOKED ME UP and down. "Celebrating Halloween a little early, are we?"

"What do you mean?"

"The duds. Normally we don't see many ninjas up this way."

"Your loss, I guess. They're big in Columbus."

"Another reason I prefer it here."

It was nearly 9:00. I'd spent the late afternoon in my motel room, squinting at my phone as I researched connections between the judge, the swamps, the contributors, PG Inc., and artificial intelligence. Bonnie was right about AI as the next big thing. I'd learned that Uber recently used a self-driving truck to make its first commercial delivery—of two thousand cases of beer. Now that was technology I could get on board with. In China, Alibaba had come up with an artificial intelligence model that did better than measly humans in a Stanford University comprehension and reading test. Meanwhile, Google was teaching machines to learn tasks on their own through neural networks, according to another article I read. It all sounded as scary as the beginning of Skynet from the *Terminator* movies, but also drove home the role these server farms played storing the massive amounts of information needed to power the supercomputers of the future. In Europe, buoyed by the success of Airbus, the European Union was investing billions in an artificial intelligence company dubbed Flota, named for *La Flota de la Plata*, the fleet that transported riches to Spain from the New World in the Age of Discovery. An appropriate company for the latest discovery age, I thought.

By prior arrangement, Gloria and I agreed I'd pick her up at her house, which turned out to be a modern-build two-story log cabin with a wraparound porch set back from the road on the outskirts of Mansfield and not all that far from the old Ohio State Penitentiary, which once housed hundreds of the state's most desperate criminals. These days tourists flocked there to see where scenes from *The Shawshank Redemption* and *Air Force One* were filmed. Oh, how the mighty have fallen. A pair of Rottweilers followed Gloria down the porch steps as she walked outside to greet me. She was wearing green camouflage pants and shirt and a pair of green trail-hiking boots. The dogs trotted across the large yard surrounding the house, watered a towering maple by the road, and sniffed the open palms I offered them.

"I appreciate that," Gloria said. "You let them come to you. A lot of people try to pet them first, which just makes them nervous. You said you have a dog?"

I said I did, if a couch-loving Labrador with gas counted. She laughed and then with a crisp voice commanded the dogs back inside. She locked up and returned to the van. She climbed into the passenger seat, looked around, and said, "You have a gun?"

"A gun? For what?"

"For in case of trouble."

"No gun."

"Why not?"

I explained about my plea bargain, the one that limited my time in a federal prison but also prevented me from carrying. "I have a baseball bat," I offered.

"That's almost worse than nothing. All right. Are you ready?"

"Ready as I'll ever be."

"I was afraid you were going to say that."

As we drove I explained about Bonnie's sleuthing, and the coincidence of people associated with PG Inc. making donations to Laura's campaign from an address that just happened to match that of Rumford Realty. I handed her the handwritten list I'd made of the six contributors that Bonnie e-mailed me. She read them aloud. "John Rolland, D. Palmer, T. Chou, James Chesser, R. Schiff, Ken Schilling."

"Recognize anyone?" I said.

"Never heard of any of them. You?"

"Came up short online. Or rather, I found lots of people with those names, but no connection to that company other than in the campaign finance filings. It was a little hard to tell on my phone. I think the one, Schiff, is a lawyer. But no surprise there, being it's a court race."

"Any connection to this judge? Porter?"

"Not that Bonnie or I could find."

"Bonnie's your girlfriend?"

I told her she wasn't, perhaps a bit too forcefully.

"Who is she then?"

"IT consultant is probably the best description." I gave her the rundown, including Bonnie's pregnancy, her passion for Roller Derby, and her relationship with Troy, who ran a business fostering dogs rescued from fighting rings and other unpleasantries. Including Rottweilers from time to time, though I left that part out. I also left out how Troy and I met—a sordid tale involving my unearthing the sexual abuse he suffered at the hands of an uncle as a boy, and which nearly destroyed him, not to mention wreck his relationship with Bonnie. It might take a couple beers to talk him through becoming a father, come to think of it.

When Gloria didn't reply, I added: "I don't have a girlfriend, in case that's what—"

"It wasn't," she said, sharply. "OK, turn up here."

A minute later I was driving down a narrow country road in nearly complete darkness, having left streetlights behind on the main road. We continued like that for five minutes, headlamps revealing tall stands of corn on either side, leaves just beginning to brown as summer wound down.

"Up here."

"Where?"

"There. And kill the lights."

I slowed, seeing nothing but corn. At the last moment a lane appeared on my right, cutting into the field like the sudden way out of a maze. I looked at Gloria and she nodded. I switched off the van's lights, carefully turned in and followed the lane for a hundred yards, the van bouncing along on the rough ground, until Gloria instructed me to stop.

"This is probably good enough."

"Good enough for what?"

"To stay hidden. This time of night, most people on that road"—she gestured behind her—"are either going too fast or are too drunk to pay much attention to farm lanes. Unless they're looking for something."

"Like us?"

"We'll be fine, as long as we're careful. Let's go."

"Yeah. About that."

"Don't tell me you're getting cold feet."

"My feet are always cold. It's a circulation thing. It's just that—"

"Just that what?"

"I think you should stay here."

"What? I thought we agreed—"

"We agreed this barn needs exploring, for all the reasons we went over. For Todd Orick's sake and maybe, who knows, for the judge's. But we, meaning you, need to be careful. Very careful, like you said. I've got a lot more leeway. I get caught and arrested, or something, it's an occupational hazard. But if you—"

"You think I'm not up for this? Is that it? Maybe because I'm a woman?"

"You can take that chip right off your shoulder and stick it, OK? What I was trying to say, was that if I get in a jam, it's more useful for both of us—and for Todd Orick, and his family—if you're not jammed up too. You see what I mean?"

She crossed her arms. "So I'm what in this scenario? A navigator?"

"If you mean the person who's always saving the captain's ass, sure."

Gloria sat silently for several seconds, the corner of her mouth twitching. I was starting to think it was sort of cute. The anger in her eyes: less so. I couldn't really blame her. She was like any good cop; her instinct was to barrel into the trouble zone with gun literally or figuratively drawn and save the day, danger to herself be damned. I waited while she thought things over. After another moment or so she relaxed.

"You're kind of a shithead, you know that?"

"It's been pointed out to me once or twice."

"I bet it has. But as my ex used to say, even shitheads get it right occasionally. OK. I'll hang back. But if there's a problem, or I get some indication things are going south, all bets are off."

"It's a deal."

WEEKS OF WARM WEATHER combined with periodic, drenching rainfalls ensured a tall crop of corn this year, which meant our progress could go undetected, at least until we reached the edges of the field closest to the barn. We crept forward, side by side and almost exactly in step, each in our own row separated by a line of thick-stalked plants. My eyes adjusted to the dark, though a light would have come in handy. But I knew it was out of the question, even assuming the barn was unoccupied and no one was around to track our progress: it would have been like sending up a flare. I was feeling as comfortable as one can about a late-night reconnoitering assignment when a sound two or three rows over froze us in our tracks. I thought about the Louisville Slugger collecting dust in my van. *That's almost worse than nothing.* Too late to find out now. I glanced at Gloria and saw her hand on her gun handle. I touched my black fanny pack with its mission-critical supply of chewing gum, duct tape, and some other things.

When nothing happened we took a couple more steps. I paused again, hearing something rustle just ahead of me. I took another step and jumped at a sound like the recording of a squeaky toy on fast forward. Recovering, I stared into the reproachful eyes of a raccoon grasping an ear of corn with its paws. It chastised me a second time with its high-pitched chitter before turning around and lumbering off through the stalky green expanse.

"Welcome to the country," Gloria whispered.

"We got just as many of those guys in the city. They're just not as sneaky."

"Shhh."

A minute later we stood just inside the far edge of the field. Ahead of us, across a strip of tall, gone-to-seed grass, loomed the dark expanse of the barn. A small, sagging roof overhung a secondary outbuilding that jutted a few feet outward from the rear of the barn, enclosed on either side but open in the front. My pig-farming uncle has a similar setup on his farm in Homer, Ohio. He uses it for equipment storage and as a place to hide from my aunt on the days she wants him to drive into town with her to buy scrapbooking supplies. Of more significance was the door in the middle of the outbuilding leading into the barn. What would I find on the other side?

"All right," I whispered. "This is it. See you in a few."

"For God's sake, please don't say, 'I'm going in.'"

"Took the words right out of my mouth," I said, emerging from the field and striding toward the barn.

25

I MADE IT SAFELY into the outbuilding without drawing gunfire or disapproval from another raccoon. I stood to the right of the door for a long minute waiting for an alarm to sound or a shotgun being racked or zombies to stagger forth from the shadows. When nothing happened, I turned and examined the door. The handle rotated, but that wasn't going to help much given the small padlock above it. A lock on the door of an abandoned barn. Interesting.

I peered inside but saw only darkness. The structure could have been filled with bales of straw and livestock and heavy weaponry, or empty as Noah's ark the day after it collided with Mount Ararat, but there was no way of knowing from my current vantage point. This was the moment of reckoning. I may not carry a gun, and the bat might be worse than nothing, but I'm not completely useless. I unzipped the fanny pack and pulled out my pick and tension wrench. I glanced back at the cornfield—I could just make out the wispy bun of Gloria's hair, assuming I wasn't seeing a corn tassel instead—turned around and went to work. The lock clicked open a minute later. I carefully slid it out of the curved staple and set it on a rough plank beside the door. I replaced the wrench in the pack and zipped it closed. I was now breaking and entering, which officially made it my problem and a no-fly zone for Gloria. I paused, bracing for an alarm. None came, which either meant it was my lucky night or the alarm was silent and I'd be lucky to leave alive. I put the thought out of my mind, reached inside, and turned the door handle.

INSIDE, I STOOD FOR a few seconds in the darkness, not moving. I listened in vain for telltale signs of another living creature, human or otherwise. Instead, I heard a faint mechanical hum. Like the lock, odd in a barn supposed to be abandoned. I took a couple more steps, careful to feel my way forward in the dark with a probing foot and hand. After a moment, satisfied I was alone for now, I pulled out my phone and turned on the flashlight, permitting myself a few seconds of low-wattage illumination.

At first I saw nothing out of the ordinary—at least for an old barn. I grew up in and around such buildings, my uncle's and others, and this had a familiar look and feel to it. The interior was open and smelled of wood, grass clippings, and gasoline. Whether that meant recent occupation was difficult to tell: those were odors that, like the detritus of an old house's long-dead occupants, could survive years of abandonment without dissipation. Directly before me sat a tractor, wide treads and chassis caked with mud and bits of grass. The mud recent? To my right stretched a series of stalls, empty now but likely once home to horses or cattle. To my left, along the opposite wall, shovels, pickaxes, hoes, and other tools hung haphazardly, sharing space with a couple of requisite antique horseshoes hung upside down for luck. I looked a little closer and saw what looked like black sheets of fine mesh covering the tools. Was someone that concerned about dust on farm implements? I added it to the list of oddities.

Slowly, tipping the phone light at a downward angle, I completed a full circuit of the interior. Back by the stalls, I peered into each in turn. I observed nothing more suspicious than a toolbox and what might have been fossilized horse apples in the first; empty white feed bags piled in a corner in the second; and a work table in the third, the top empty, cluttered with neither nails nor broken C-clamps or any of the hundred other bits of junk you'd expect to find. Strange in an old barn, but good housekeeping wasn't anything to base a search warrant on.

I stepped back and was deciding how to proceed when a skittering in a far corner of the last stall caused me to freeze in my tracks for the second time that night. A mouse, probably, but possibly a rat, depending on how much spilled grain was left around the place. I thought fleetingly of the judge's cat, lounging in my house with Hopalong, its new BFF, and wondered if it had ever been outside. The overnight accommodation of cats was a running debate between my parents as my sister and I were growing up. My mom was opposed to letting them inside except for the most bitter January and February nights—and even then confined only to the chilly mud room—content to let them hang out year-round in the small barn on our property. My father, who had a soft spot for animals which got softer the more beers he consumed, would regularly sneak them inside and then feign ignorance at their appearance atop the dining room table where my mother was trying to grade papers after dinner. There was this one time—

The skittering again. Carefully, I crept back into the stall to see if I could find the source of the sound. I didn't see rodents of any stripe, but I observed something I missed the first time: a thick orange extension cord running from the bottom edge of the work table across the floor.

I ILLUMINATED THE SPACE with my phone, holding it up higher to disperse the light farther. The table sat in front of me, top just above waist level, but I saw now that what I'd taken for an empty surface was in fact a large sheet of green canvas. I listened for a moment, and realized the electrical hum I heard earlier was coming from inside this small space.

Assuring myself again that I was still alone, I approached the table, reached out, and touched the canvas. I felt the slightest vibration. A sickening feeling swept through my stomach, as when you realize a lie you've told is about to be exposed for all and sundry to hear. I knew that vibration. I'd felt it many times, running to the basement as a kid on my mom's instructions to find something for dinner. I knotted the canvas in my right hand and pulled. It took a moment, because the canvas was big and heavy, like the material Boy Scouts used to erect tents in the pre–nylon pop-up days. But in a few seconds I had the covering off and piled on the floor. Before me sat a large, white freezer chest. Long and more than deep enough to hold . . .

I swallowed, preparing for the worst. To hold Todd Orick? A kid dumb enough to go fishing on the morning of his girlfriend's birthday, but just smart enough to plan on taking her to brunch afterward, even if it was Down Home Buffet and not someplace fancy, like Bob Evans. Brunch plans interrupted, perhaps forever? But what if it wasn't Todd? What if—

I thought of the night I met the judge at the Christmas party hosted by Burke Cunningham. How attractive I found her—no surprise, given her patrician looks, confident bearing, and tastefully conservative dress—yet also how aloof and unapproachable she seemed. An aloofness that underscored the surprise I felt when she called a couple of days later and asked if I was available for an assignment. I thought of our subsequent Sunday morning appointments in her condo, the flashes of passion she exhibited in a rare and private departure from a rule-driven existence about as exotic as the leather-bound law books on the shelves of her home office. Thought of the reminder of that passion I tasted in her car outside my house two nights earlier, how soft her lips were, right before she took a phone call that led to her abrupt departure and mysterious disappearance.

My God—are you all right?

Who called her? And why? What scared her so badly?

I stopped myself. There was no point. I took a breath, stepped forward and opened the freezer door, blinking as an interior light illuminated the darkened stall. I gasped, unable to help myself, staring at the freezer's contents in disbelief.

26

THE FREEZER WAS FILLED with dead birds. Birds of all shapes and sizes and species, piled one on top of another in frozen clumps, rimmed with faint patterns of frost. A grotesque conglomeration of wings, beaks, feathers, feet, and dull eyes staring at me like tarnished baubles. I had never seen anything like it in my life.

I reached inside, tugged gently at the nearest one until it loosened enough to pull free in my hand without too much damage. I examined it in the light provided by the freezer. It was a black bird of some kind. A starling or grackle or even small crow, one of the jillions of similar-looking birds you took for granted every day—"little black jobbers," my sister called them—seeing them swirl in shape-shifting clouds in the sky or perched on tree branches, twittering in a raucous chorus in the late afternoon or early evening. I replaced it and carefully pried loose another. This one I easily recognized as a robin. I set it back and retrieved a sparrow, then another robin, then a bright red cardinal. It was the one I pulled out next that gave me pause.

At first I mistook it for a finch of some kind because of the color on its wings and back feathers. The two Kevins grew sunflowers along their alley-facing fence that attracted finches in droves each summer. My bird-watching normally started and ended with observations of the fluttering creatures as I lounged in my Adirondack with a beer and a book in the backyard. But even I could tell this bird was bigger than any finch I'd ever seen. I'd also never seen finches with streaks of orange like this one sported, a color that brought to mind of all things the shade of the Cleveland Browns' uniforms. An oriole, perhaps? Yet that didn't seem right either. I thought absentmindedly of the rare bird that summered at Mendon Woods in Columbus—coastal something. But why would it be here? Puzzled, I set this one on the floor beside me and continued digging, curious how many birds the freezer actually held. And also to address the tiny bit of dread still gripping my stomach that the birds might be covering up something else, something—or someone?

I needn't have worried. It was birds all the way to the bottom.

I pulled my hands out of the freezer and rubbed them back and forth for warmth before continuing my investigation. After a minute I reached back in and pried loose more birds. Another black bird. A sparrow, then an actual finch, then a bluebird, then another of the colorful orange birds. I thought of my animal-loving dad, sitting at the breakfast table in the kitchen, watching birds attack the suet bags he hung in the apple tree. Chances are he might know. I'd take a picture when I was finished, get it to him and see what he said. I reached down again, touching the freezer's bottom, feeling my phone vibrate as I did. Multiple buzzes signifying a call. I stood and slipped the phone from my pocket. I didn't recognize the number. I disconnected. But as I did, I saw I'd missed two texts from the same number, a minute apart.

We've got company

Get out of there

Gloria. Shit.

I carefully dropped the freezer door and draped the canvas back over the appliance, making sure it lay exactly as I found it. I reached down, grabbed the bird I'd liberated from the freezer— I'd call it a Browns warbler for now—and tucked it into my hoodie's front pocket, just in time to hear the sound of the door at the front of the barn rolling open.

27

PRAYING THAT MY ALL-BLACK purchases at Walmart hadn't been in vain, I ducked my head, channeled my inner ninja, and dashed from the stall to the tractor. Just in time I slid behind the large rear wheel facing the door through which I'd entered minutes earlier. I held my breath. So far, so good. I heard low voices, men's, not two dozen yards away. Shadows danced on the walls as flashlight beams crisscrossed back and forth. I listened closely.

"They'll be here soon. Hurry the fuck up."

"Calm down. It's at least an hour from Columbus."

Voices of men going about their business, however mysterious. But what business? And who will be here soon? At least they weren't the voices of men searching for an intruder. Small difference, in a space that enclosed, but it gave me the slightest advantage. My phone buzzed again. I glanced at the message.

I'm coming in

I thought of the freezer, and the puzzle of the birds inside. Its significance as an indicator of something strange going on. The judge's admonition: *no police*. Gloria's fear of local corruption. It came to me all at once. We couldn't blow our cover yet. We didn't know what we didn't know, but we'd never know anything if the two men a fraction of a furlong away realized they'd been compromised.

No wait I texted back, thankful for the flashlight beams, which meant the light from my phone would go undetected.

Why??

I lowered myself until I had an unobstructed view under the tractor's undercarriage. The two were now in the stall with the freezer. Even with their backs turned, I recognized one as Tear Drop. The other was taller and wider. They had the door open and appeared to be prying birds free. I turned around and glanced at the door I'd come through. I could cover the short distance quickly, but it was almost guaranteed the sound would give me away. I turned around, crouching behind the tractor's back wheel.

Carefully, I tapped, *Need distraction but not rescue*

A few seconds passed. No reply. A few more seconds, then nearly a minute. Nothing. Which could mean almost anything, starting with her phone died and proceeding quickly to Gloria was in trouble herself, maybe busted, maybe worse. Which meant I was on my own. I waited another minute, pocketed the phone, and counted the steps I needed to move from tractor to my exit. The problem was opening and closing the door, which no matter how carefully I managed it would give me away as surely as if I stood up and sang "Carmen Ohio" at the top of my lungs.

"What was that?"

One of the voices. Tear Drop, if I wasn't mistaken. *You're dead.*

"What?"

"I thought I heard something."

"Like what?"

"Like I'm not sure. Over there someplace."

"You're imagining things."

"I don't think so. Hang on a second."

So much for keeping our cover. I bounced up and down on my knees, ready to run. Three, two, one—

Thud.

Something struck the front corner of the barn hard, by the open door where the two men entered a few minutes ago, sending a shudder through the building.

"What the fuck?"

Tear Drop. Flashlight beams bobbed and danced away from me, toward the impact.

I ran. Crouching, I covered the short distance, pulled open the door, moved outside, slowly, slowly drew the door shut, picked up the lock from the shelf, clasped it through the hasp, clicked it closed, turned and dashed into the cornfield.

I STOPPED HALFWAY ACROSS to catch my breath and listen for pursuers. Instead, I heard a commotion outside on the other side of the barn, a two-man chorus of "fucks" and "shits" filling the night air. I wasn't sure what was going on. But I wasn't being chased, and I was out of the barn safely. The more important question was: Where the hell was Gloria?

I was interrupted by the sound of someone running hard down a row of corn, straight toward me. I braced myself for an assault, regretting my Louisville Slugger one last time. Big help the chewing gum in the fanny pack would be. The footsteps grew closer, coming fast. Closer, and closer still—

"*Shit!*" Gloria hissed as she stumbled into view, losing her balance at the sight of me and knocking me down as she fell over.

"What the—" I said, moving to untangle ourselves.

"*Shhh,*" she said, going still atop me. Near enough that I could feel her heart pounding in her chest.

"What the hell's going on?"

"*Shut up.*"

We lay like that for a count of ten, me on my back, Gloria lying on top of me, both our heads turned toward the barn, listening. That close, her camouflage smelled of wood smoke, bug spray, and an odor it took me a second to identify—a rub-on deer-urine scent. Between that and her disguise, it would have been love at first sight if I'd had a rack of antlers and a ruminating stomach.

"All right," she said after another moment. "Let's go."

She rolled off, got to her knees, and stood. She glanced back toward the barn through the stalks of corn, reached a hand down, and pulled me up. I followed her through the cornfield. To my amazement, the shouts on the other side of the barn had turned to laughter. A minute later we were at the van. I put it in reverse, backed up as quickly as possible without leaving my transmission behind as a souvenir, and retraced my route up the dark country road.

28

"ALEXA," GLORIA SAID. "WHAT kind of bird is this?"

"I'm not sure that's something I can help with."

"Why the hell not?"

"There's no reason to swear, Gloria."

"Wanna bet?"

We were sitting at Gloria's dining room table half an hour later, our right hands each clamped around a bottle of Great Lakes Dortmunder Gold. The Browns warbler sat on a plate between us, glistening as it defrosted. The Rottweilers dozed on the pine-planked floor on either side of Gloria's brown Windsor wood chair. The dogs' names were Carl and Madeleine. Asleep they looked like brown hillocks. I was careful to do that thing where you let them lie.

I said, "I wouldn't have pegged you as a digital assistant kind of gal."

"And why's that?"

"No offense. I was just thinking you'd go with more of a full-fledged android type servant. Like RoboCop or something."

"RoboCop wasn't an android. He was a cyborg. And too high-maintenance, you ask me. No offense taken, I guess. My daughter got it for me for Christmas. I would have stuck it in a drawer, but it makes my grandkids laugh. They like talking to it. My granddaughter accidentally ordered a stuffed horse last month. Thanks, Amazon. Of course I didn't have the heart to send it back."

"I also wouldn't have pegged you as a grandmother."

"Oh, really?"

"You don't look that old—and don't try to deny it," I said, waving off the objection I saw forming on her lips. "You also don't act that old, judging by your ability to break into locked vans during a late-night ops maneuver."

"Unlocked vans, thank you very much."

"Really?"

"Who'd lock a van like that in the middle of the country?"

I had to admit the distraction Gloria came up with was clever. After sneaking up, she'd opened the driver's door, placed the van in neutral, and rocked it forward. Gravity and momentum did the rest. The van traveled thirty yards down a slope before colliding with the corner of the building. If we were lucky, the obscenities I heard from the safety of the cornfield were the two men blaming the other for not leaving the van in park, followed by ribbing as each accused the other of being a dipshit.

"You saved our bacon, that's for sure. However old you are."

"Thank you, I suppose. Forty-seven next month. I married young and divorced young. Like you, right?"

"Let me guess—Wikipedia?"

She colored slightly. "I looked you up last year, after . . . after Red, White & Boom. I don't think I was alone, by the way."

"That explains my three extra Twitter followers. So—what the hell was that back there, in the barn? And what's this?" I nodded at the bird.

"And who's coming from Columbus?" she said.

"All good questions. Makes me think we should pay a return visit?"

"And jinx ourselves? I don't think so."

"But what if it's the judge?" I had an uneasy feeling in my stomach.

"That doesn't make sense, Hayes. Didn't you say she must have taken off two nights ago?"

"I suppose you're right. Still be nice to know what they were talking about."

"Agreed. I can swing by there tomorrow. But that reminds me—I almost forgot." She reached into the back pocket of her camouflage pants and retrieved a sliver of white cardboard. "I found this on the floor of the driver's seat of the van."

I took the paper from her. A torn business card, minus the name of the person it belonged to. What was left were fragments of a job title—. . . *ney-at-law*—the partial name of a law-firm-y sounding company—. . . *Northcott, Rickard and Dowd*—and an address in Cleveland on Euclid Avenue.

"Evidence collection on the fly. Nice job."

"Cop, remember?"

I pulled out my phone and looked up the address. Sure enough, a law firm. Full name: Raabe, Karabinus, Northcott, Rickard and Dowd. None of them meant anything to me.

"Whoever's card this is—the boss of those two guys in the barn?" Gloria said.

"Hard to say, just based on that."

"But connected?"

"Has to be, I'm thinking. I mean, what isn't at this point?"

She nodded and drained the shoulders from her beer. She pushed her chair back and walked into the kitchen. The hillocks rose in unison and click-clicked after her. She opened a cupboard door, removed a bag of pretzels, and tore open the top. She reached up and retrieved a wooden salad bowl from the other side of the cupboard. She dumped the pretzels in and returned to the table. She placed the bowl between us. The hillocks renewed their sentry duty, signaling their battle-readiness with perfectly matched snores. Gloria and I reached for pretzels at the same time, touched hands, withdrew them quickly.

"So this freezer," she said. "Completely full of birds?"

"More or less."

"But only a few like this?"

Keeping an eye on Gloria's hands, I freed a fistful of pretzels from their captivity and popped a couple into my mouth.

"More than a few. Less than a flock."

"Fact they were frozen means somebody wants them preserved, obviously."

"Maybe. But why? And where are they from?"

"Could be anywhere. But that close to Heyder's Creek? Swamp's as good a guess as any. Lots of birds in there."

"What happened to them, do you think? Disease?"

She shook her head. "Someone caught 'em, you ask me. That's a basically healthy-looking bird, whatever it is."

It was then that I recalled the bird from Mendon Woods in Columbus. Coastal . . . tanager. I did a search on my phone. I pulled up the result, examined it and showed Gloria.

"That could be it, though it's hard to tell. This one's in rough shape."

"Injured when it was caught?"

"I doubt it," Gloria said. "We get biologists from the Ohio State campus in Mansfield from time to time, tagging birds. They throw these mesh nets up to catch them. But they're tagging 'em, not killing them, and they're fine afterward." She used the base of her beer bottle to nudge the bird. "This one looks like its neck was broken."

Mesh nets. I related what I'd seen draped over the tools on the barn wall.

"But why catch and kill them?" I said.

"I don't know. And I don't know if it's related to Todd Orick either. But it's damned strange."

"Yes, it is. I might know somebody who could help us, though."

"Who?"

I took a couple of pictures of the bird from different angles and texted them to my mom. After they went through I added a message.

Can you ask dad if he knows what kind of bird this is?

Why? she texted back almost immediately. She was up late as usual, likely reading or watching TV. I could guarantee my father was already dead asleep.

Just curious. I'll talk to you tomorrow.

I explained to Gloria what I'd done.

"Is he a birder?"

"More or less. But he'd never call himself one."

"Why not?"

"It would make him think of environmentalists or something, who he despises, even though he spends half his time bitching about the way development is screwing up rural Ohio. But yeah, he birds. Mainly from his kitchen window, but sometimes in the woods too, when no one's looking."

"Sounds like my mom and her pills. She's always complaining about the cost of health care and how the insurance companies are sticking it to her. But suggest Obamacare might not be a bad thing? She'd sooner see you in hell."

"To birders and Obamacare." I raised my bottle and we clinked glass. I ate a couple more pretzels and finished my beer in two swigs. I pushed back my chair and stood. "All right. This has been real, but it's late, and I assume you have to work tomorrow. I'll let you know what my dad says. Then I'll figure out my next move."

"Where are you going?"

"Find a place to stay, I guess. Motel 6 isn't the only game in town, from what I could tell."

"I'm not sure that's such a good idea."

"Why not?"

"Don't you get it, Hayes? You forgetting your slashed tires?"

"What about them?"

"You're not just a pretty face anymore—you're a made man in this town, buster."

29

I SAT DOWN AND helped myself to another handful of pretzels. Gloria followed suit, each of us carefully choreographing the timing of our reach.

I said, "What are you talking about?"

"Think about it. I've got my chief plus the Mohican County sheriff waving me off stuff related to Todd's disappearance. So that tells you something right there. Then you show up and yours is the only vehicle at the Motel 6 with complimentary tire slashing. That's when I figured—"

"Figured what?"

"That you weren't, you know, a baddie."

"A baddie? What is this, *Murder She Wrote*?"

"Fine—a fucking baddie. You know what I mean."

"But you already knew who I was. From—"

"From Red, White & Boom. Yeah, I knew. And I wanted to believe you weren't on the dark side, trust me. And I got my wish, sorry for the loss of your tires."

"Thanks, I think."

"They bought the ruse with their van tonight, as far as I can tell. But either way, whatever's going on, whoever's involved, the alarms are sounding. Mohican Township's a small burg. You're a wanted man now. Maybe you could find another motel, get a good night sleep followed by a tasty continental breakfast. Or maybe not. You want to risk that?"

"I see your point. But what are my options? Drive back to Columbus? Whatever's going on with the judge, it looks connected to stuff here, not there. I'm not ready to beat a retreat quite yet."

"Just stay here," she said, not meeting my eyes. "Bunk on the couch. I'll stand you a spare toothbrush and a phone charger if you ask nicely. We can figure out next steps in the morning."

"You sure?"

She nodded. "You just need to move your van."

"Why?"

"Where it's parked right now it's visible from the road. I thought of that once we came inside. We've already run the risk someone's seen it, though I'm guessing we're OK since nobody's launching grenades our way. Just pull it around back, next to the shed. There's nothing but woods behind me."

"All right. If you're really—"

"Just move the van, Hayes."

I excused myself and walked outside. Looking up, I realized how fitting my all-black getup was given how dark it was. Constellations dusted the sky like a billion pinpricks of oncoming traffic on the world's darkest superhighway, the stars clearer and brighter than I'd seen in years. All the growth in Columbus was good for the economy but lousy for stargazing. I started the van and followed Gloria's instructions, pulling back around behind the house next to a shed large enough to hold a mower, tools, and a couple ponies, if it came to that. I walked around to the rear, opened the Odyssey's trunk, retrieved the go bag, locked up, and went back inside.

"Hey—check this out."

Gloria had relocated into her living room, where she sat on a long, brown leather couch—my bunk, presumably—laptop on her knees, fingers working the touchpad. The bowl of pretzels had also migrated and was now sitting on the polished wood slab coffee table in front of her. Beside it sat two fresh Dortmunder

Golds. Across the room, the hillocks snoozed beside a stone hearth fireplace.

I sat beside her and grabbed a beer. "What?"

"The names of the donors to your judge? The one your preggers IT buddy found?"

"What about them?"

"Well, I looked up the firm whose name was on the card in the van. You can search the website. I put all six names from that list in. Guess what?"

"A match?"

"Only one. But it looks good. R. Schiff. Or Randall P. Schiff, if it's the same guy."

"Good work." I explained how that name had shown up twice—once under PG Inc., once by himself during the primary giving cycle.

"Well, here he is."

I leaned closer as we examined the results.

He was thin, with the angular face of a guy who takes the gym seriously, strong chin, eyes the color of the Caribbean bays where men like that keep sailboats, pleasant smile, cropped hair turned prematurely white. According to his profile, he specialized in real estate law with subspecialties in transactional documentation, sale of equity interests, and annexation disputes, whatever any of that meant. No indication he used *estoppel* in everyday conversation. Raabe, Karabinus, Northcott, Rickard and Dowd looked high end, no question. All of this was interesting, though none of it meant much by itself: there were three chartered buses full of lawyers like Schiff in every big city in America. What did catch my attention was his educational background. Law degree from Ohio State, Juris Doctor awarded the same year Laura Porter earned her own JD there.

"Do you mind if I check something?"

"Be my guest."

She slid the laptop over. I hunted and pecked for the website for the auditor of Cuyahoga County, which surrounds Cleveland.

It only took a minute of searching. As you would expect for a lawyer with that kind of profile, Schiff wasn't doing too badly, as measured by the cost of his home in the small city of Bay Front, located west of Cleveland and hugging the coastline of Lake Erie like an elongated bag of money: $2.4 million at construction, recently appraised at $2.65 million.

"He must make serious bank," Gloria said.

"Why my father wished I'd gone into transactional documentation."

"Which begs the question," she continued. "What's the torn-up business card of a stinking-rich lawyer doing in the van of a couple of guys skulking around a decrepit barn containing a freezer full of dead birds on the edge of a swamp?"

"If you put it that way. Plus, how big a coincidence is it that he was in law school at the same time as Laura?"

"Who?"

"The judge I told you about."

"Another good question."

"One which I'll add to the list." I opened a new tab, pulled up Nexis, entered my user name and password, and did some quick backgrounding. Schiff had previous addresses in Shaker Heights on Cleveland's east side. I checked associated addresses. A couple relatives—mom or aunt—with the same last name. Likely where he grew up—not an unexpected pedigree for a corporate lawyer in Cleveland. I examined neighbors whose names didn't mean anything to me, except one: Samuel Northcott. Same as the name on the firm's masthead? Or another coincidence? I did a quick check—yes, now retired partner in the firm. It's all in who you know, I guess. I looked in vain for any connection between Schiff and Laura beyond Ohio State. I noticed another related address, in Parma, another Cleveland suburb, and did some Googling, starting to feel excited as though I'd found something significant. But it turned out Schiff also owned an apartment complex, which I guess made sense for someone in real estate. Frustrated, I logged out and slid the laptop back to Gloria. She set it atop the coffee table.

"Any of that mean anything?" she said.

"Who knows? Colonel Northcott in the legal library with the gavel—or squat. Impossible to tell at this point."

I reached for my beer and put the upper third out of its misery. I replaced the bottle on the table and reached for more pretzels, just as Gloria did.

"Hayes."

"What?"

"You're in my way."

"Sorry—"

"Don't."

"Don't what?"

"Don't be sorry. And don't remove your hand."

"If I don't remove my hand, our fingers will remain in contact. Amidst the pretzels."

"An astute observation. Of course, you're a trained investigator."

"Takes one to know one."

We were looking at each other now, eyes searching the other's face. The corner of her mouth twitched. Yup, no question. It was cute.

"Was that a dig?"

"A compliment," I said. "You connected some major dots in this case in the time it took me to go outside and move my van."

"And come back inside with an overnight bag, I noticed."

"It's a go bag. It's for emergencies. For things that crop up at the last second that you weren't expecting."

"Isn't that what 911 is for?"

"Depends on the emergency."

She leaned close. I leaned closer. We repeated the drill and I kissed her. I tasted pretzels and beer and smelled wood smoke and bug spray and rub-on deer-urine scent. These are a few of my favorite things.

"Ever done it with a grandma, Hayes?" she said after a minute.

"Not to the best of my recollection."

"We take a little longer. I hope that's OK."

"Take as long as you need."

"Alexa," Gloria said. "Play some Reba McEntire. Slow stuff."

"I thought you said she was just for your grandkids."

"My house. My rules."

"I can live with that."

"*Here's what I found,*" Alexa replied, as the music began to play.

30

THE GRAY LIGHT OF dawn was filtering into the room when my eyes opened the next morning. Gloria lay asleep beside me, face planted on her pillow. I was very much not on the couch. I eased up as quietly as possible from her bed and set feet on floor. Gloria stirred, tugging at the sheet, but didn't awaken. I reached out for my phone and checked the time. Not quite six. I had texts from both Kevin M. and Bonnie. Bonnie's said, Check your e-mail. Carefully, maneuvering my way past a pair of slumbering Rottweilers, I retrieved my clothes and tiptoed out of the room.

I pulled my spare kit from the go bag and tiptoed into the bathroom. A few minutes later, I crept into the kitchen and after a couple false starts found what I needed to make coffee. While it brewed I opened the text from Kevin M. He'd sent three pictures: another of Hopalong at Schiller Park with the pugs; a second of what appeared to be a rack of ribs from Kevin H.'s new smoker; and a third, somewhat to my astonishment, of Laura's cat nestled beside Hopalong on my couch as the two dozed. Will wonders never cease. As the coffee dripped, I read the e-mail from Bonnie.

She'd done some additional research on PG Inc. and the other donors on the list she sent me. Some of them showed up in references to a giant server farm project in Indiana that had apparently floundered. Flota, the European Union–backed AI rival to Google and Amazon, was the company behind the deal. That made sense, as Bonnie noted: Flota had projects on the front burner in Germany, Sweden, and Estonia, which was embarked on a project to transform itself into a completely digital society. Communities were bending over backward to woo these companies, with billions on the line in terms of construction spending, not to mention the impact of thousands of new employees on a community.

That's the funny thing about AI, Bonnie wrote. It takes a lot of humans to make it work.

She added: If PG Inc. is connected to Flota, I'm guessing it has plenty of money to make big donations to your judge, for what it's worth.

Three beeps in sequence signaled the completion of the coffee. I opened and shut cupboards until I found a mug collection. I considered my options, settled on one that said Richland County FOP, filled it, and retreated to the couch. I snapped on a light and pulled Gloria's laptop off the coffee table and onto my lap. I brought it to life, but it asked for a password immediately. Duh. Cop. I replaced it, allowed myself ten seconds of further self-recrimination for setting out on this misadventure without my own computer, and returned to my phone.

I tried combining Laura's name and PG Inc. and Flota in Google searches, with no luck. So whatever the connection was between someone named Randall P. Schiff and Laura and these companies—if there even was a connection—someone was keeping a lid on it. Yet Schiff and the judge shared a bond that was undeniable: attendance at the same law school. Where they had to have known each other, despite the size of the class. I thought back to the judge's home office and the trashed Berman Prize certificate. Was that related somehow?

I sat back, took a sip of coffee, and reviewed what I knew about the judge's past, almost none of which I learned from her despite the amount of time we'd been together, however you defined that. Instead, over the years I pieced things together the old-fashioned way: via the internet and courthouse gossip.

Laura grew up in modest means on the west side of Columbus, her father one of the last people to earn a full-time paycheck from the old Delphi plant, where Hollywood Casino now stood. Talk about the fallen mighty. Her mother was a homemaker who eventually returned to the workforce, helping keep the books at Haydocy Buick down the street from Delphi. There was never any question Laura was going to college; there was also never any question, especially after her father was laid off, that she would attend Ohio State. To her parents' dismay she majored in political science instead of something practical—meaning something that would provide a steady income upon graduation—and grew interested in the law. She considered other places for law school, but in the end decided to stay right where she was.

But why? I knew she was considered a bit of a wunderkind in college. Working-class girl made good and all that. Grades through the roof. She could have had her pick of blue-chip law schools. Why stay here, apart from Ohio State's overall strong reputation?

Once again I thought of the broken frame in the wastepaper basket with its shards of shattered glass, each like a translucent knife capable of drawing blood. I picked up my phone, pulled up the browser icon, and typed "Ohio State law school Berman Prize." I waited for the results, held the phone closer, and read.

> Awarded annually to the top Ohio applicant, the Berman Prize provides full tuition reimbursement and a stipend for all three years of study for candidates pursuing their Juris Doctor degree at the Moritz College of Law at The Ohio State University.

I skimmed the details. The prize was prestigious, to say the least, since for starters it guaranteed a practically debt-free beginning to your legal career. It was named for a local lawyer who'd grown up on a farm and worked his way through both undergraduate work and a law degree at Ohio State while still arising at 4 a.m. to milk the family dairy herd. After graduation, he went on to found one of the city's oldest and most powerful law firms. As a result, the prize had a utilitarian side to it as a carrot to keep homegrown stars home. And, perhaps its strongest suit, the Berman Prize balanced the carrot of generosity with a stick of standards. Winners had to maintain a minimum GPA of 3.5, undertake pro bono projects even during the school year, and spend one summer working in a public interest legal position. Fail to meet any of those requirements and the prize—and the scholarship money—was rescinded. I was pretty sure Laura's public interest stint was an internship with the Justice Department, one of the highest-profile positions you could land as a law student. A job that helped launch her career after graduation, first as an assistant U.S. attorney for the Southern District of Ohio, where she earned a reputation for fearless prosecutions of drug dealers, identity thieves, wannabe terrorists, and any other bad guys that crossed her path. The beginnings of the Velvet Fist, no doubt. Then later as a judge, handily winning her first election. But some of these details were fuzzy. I had a contact at the U.S. Attorney's Office who might know more—that is, I knew one AUSA who wouldn't hang up on me immediately, thanks to owing me a favor or two. I made a mental note to call him later.

Along the way Laura married Paul Thayer, a fellow law school student. They had two kids, a son and a daughter—I recalled again the photo by her bedside—and bought a house in the tony suburb of Upper Arlington with a white picket fence undoubtedly made of solid silver. Figuratively speaking, about as far from the blue-collar west side of Columbus as you could go. Laura's life was the success her hardworking parents always wished for her.

And then after a few years her husband came to the tried-and-true conclusion that a firm associate with firm thighs and zero stretch marks was the person who truly completed him, and Laura's world came tumbling down in the blink of a breakfast-table announcement. In the aftermath of Paul's departure, the only companionship she tolerated was a bodyguard type with no strings attached whom she invited into her bed once a week.

Until he decided a few strings might not be such a bad thing, and that went out the window too. All well and good. Actually, complicated as hell.

The question was, what did fellow law school classmate Randall P. Schiff, a bunch of dead birds, and a cloud-computing company with links to a European artificial intelligence giant have to do with any of it?

And where the hell was Laura?

31

A TOILET FLUSHING AT the back of the house interrupted my musings. I heard water running in a sink, followed by the tread of footsteps and the click-click of canine nails. Movement in the kitchen, a cupboard door opening and closing. The clunk of a coffee pot pulled from its base and replaced a moment later. A minute after that Gloria appeared in the living room, trailed by Carl and Madeleine. Gloria was in purple slippers, wearing black sweatpants and a loose-fitting Mansfield Tygers T-shirt. She turned a dining-room chair to face me and sat.

"Good morning, Hayes."

"Morning."

"Toilet seat down and fresh coffee. I'm impressed. Solid B-plus."

"B-plus?"

"You stole the covers. Plus you snore like a truck going off a cliff."

"Sorry about that. I'm told it's related to how many times my nose has been broken."

"And how many times would that be?"

"My accountant's still running the numbers."

"Too many, I'm guessing. You're up early. What are you working on?"

I explained what Bonnie sent about PG Inc. and Flota and the failed Indiana project. Then I explained my research on the judge and the Berman Prize and my feeling that some element of the mystery had to lie in the past, with the judge and Schiff's time at law school.

She sipped her coffee. "Maybe they were involved? A spurned-lover thing."

"Maybe. I'm not sure the judge was focused much on romance in those days." I told her about the scholarship's rigorous requirements.

"You seem to know a lot about this judge."

"Trained investigator. Remember?"

"Oh, I remember. Believe me. It's just that I have a different theory."

"OK."

"I'm a trained investigator, too, as you noted. And I'm considering the fact you had a key to this judge's condo, which sounds a little peculiar to me. Add to that the amount of energy you're expending to find her—"

"I told you—"

"All of which makes me think, if this IT lady who's helping you out isn't your girlfriend, maybe this judge is. Which is an interesting way to look at a lot of things, don't you think?"

"The judge isn't—"

"Isn't what?"

A good question. I thought of Laura's and my encounter in her Lexus. The fire of old passion temporarily revived, followed almost immediately by the chilling effect of the phone call.

"She's not my girlfriend, all right? But gold star on your forehead for your instincts. She was, in a manner of speaking, once upon a time. But that's been a while now."

"A manner of speaking? What the hell is that supposed to mean?"

"It means things were complicated between us and ended badly. So badly I hadn't spoken to her in five years until she called out of the blue three days ago. The fact she called me as opposed to anyone else, including anybody with a badge, makes me think she might be in real trouble. That's why I'm feeling so involved."

"No other reason?"

"Are you asking if I still have feelings for her? Yes. No. Maybe. Does it matter? I'm not really sure. Don't tell me in your job you don't run into complicated relationships."

She didn't respond for a moment. She took another drink of coffee. She reached down to scratch Madeleine on the head. Or maybe it was Carl.

"That brings up something else."

"OK."

"Last night. I mean—"

My turn to drink coffee. No dog to scratch, so I ran my hand through my hair.

"I don't want you to get the wrong impression. That I was—"

"That you were what?"

She looked away. "That I was thanking you, or something."

"Thanking me? For what?"

"Thanking you for saving my son's life. And his girlfriend's. I mean, I am grateful. I can't tell you how much. But I just don't want you to think that I'd—"

"I don't think that."

"And I also want to make it clear—"

Scratch. Tail thump. Scratch. Tail thump.

"The thing is, I'm settled here. Comfortable—it's home. Always has been. My grandkids are here. My daughter and her husband live fifteen minutes away, in town."

"What do they do?"

"She works part-time at a craft store, but mostly she's home with the kids. He's a guard at Mansfield Correctional. I'm just not—"

"I get it, don't worry. I don't have grandkids, at least that I know of, but I know what my mom would say if my boys lived any farther away than they do now. My dad, for that matter. I appreciate your help with this case. And I appreciated sleeping someplace besides the couch last night."

"Thanks, Hayes. I appreciated that too. Just because I'm OK being alone doesn't mean I don't get lonely."

"So now that we've got that worked out—"

Before I could continue I was interrupted by "Welcome to the Jungle" pulsing from my phone on the coffee table. Ignoring Gloria's eye roll, I retrieved it and answered.

"Mom?"

"That's a coastal tanager."

My father's voice.

"Sorry—I thought you were Mom. What did you say?"

"The bird. That picture you sent."

"What about it?"

"It's a coastal tanager. It's one of the rarest birds in North America. Really, in the world."

32

I RAISED A FOREFINGER at Gloria, signaling I needed to stay on the call. She nodded and walked into the kitchen, Carl and Madeleine in close pursuit. A moment later I heard the sound of kibble rattling into metal bowls.

"How do you know this?" I said to my father.

"I've read some stuff, OK? Thing is, you hardly ever see 'em in Ohio anymore. Why's that one dead? Don't tell me you hit it with that van of yours."

"It was dead when I found it." I heard the sound of a machine in the background. "Where are you?"

"Wiggins's. Where are you?"

"Wiggins's? Why?"

"I work here."

Of course. I'd forgotten that my dad had landed a job at a local hardware store near Homer, finally holding down regular work again at a time in life most guys his age have retired and then some. He was off the booze at last—thanks in part to a come-to-Jesus moment a few years back surviving a heart attack. At the store, he'd shown himself an able and affable employee, his never-met-a-stranger demeanor perfect for the small-town establishment.

"Right. You're there early."

"Always am. Where are you?" he repeated.

I glanced into the kitchen. Gloria was at the counter, setting something on plates. I let my eyes linger on her backside for a moment. "Out of town. Why are you using Mom's phone?"

"I left before she was up, so she came by the store. Showed me the pictures you sent. Made it seem like it was important. If it's not, no big deal," he said, sharpness creeping into his voice. "I don't have to—"

"It is important, and I really appreciate it," I interrupted, eager to keep things on an even keel. My dad had mellowed in recent years, but some things remained the same, and one of them was a quick-to-the-trigger temper when he felt underappreciated. Not that our relationship was a whole lot easier these days. He was an avid Trump supporter, and the argument-slash-shouting match we had over some presidential tweet or another not long ago resulted in my mom's banning all conversation about politics until future notice. Left to talk about farming and sports, we might not do much better, but at least we'd be speaking to each other at the end of the evening.

I said, "I don't know how this bird died, though I'm trying to find out. It's connected to an investigation."

"What kind of investigation?"

"Missing-person case. Just routine."

"A missing-person case with a dead coastal tanager? Doesn't sound routine to me."

"That's why I was trying to find out what kind of bird it is." I explained how I'd dubbed it a Browns warbler because of its splashes of orange.

"Might as well name a bird after the Browns. About all they're going to be known for. Biggest bunch of losers I ever saw. I mean, they were bad when you played up there, but at least you won a couple games."

"Anything else you can tell me about this bird?" I said, eager to change the subject. Allowing Bud Hayes to venture down the path of my squandered football career was the conversational equivalent of tossing a lighted stick of dynamite back and forth.

"Coastal tanager—which coast?"

"Brazil. They summer up here."

"Starting when?"

"April, maybe May. Used to be gone by October, but now you see them a little later into the fall, all this weird weather we've been having."

"Weird weather" the code my dad used to signal his complete and utter disregard for any suggestion that climate change was real. I'd taken the bait in the past, to my regret. Another landmine to step around.

"I appreciate you letting me know," I said. "It's very helpful. And I'm grateful to Mom for running down there with the phone. Is she there?"

"She's talking to Henry. Why?"

Henry Wiggins, the store owner, was one of the few people in Homer, Ohio, willing to give my dad a second chance—well, third or fourth—after all his problems. It was a courtesy that diehard Buckeyes fan had never afforded me, not that I was counting. In this state, even two decades or so after I cost the school a national championship, you had to take a ticket to join the club of people who hated my guts.

"No reason. I just wanted to thank her. I hope you have a good day."

"I hope I do too." He disconnected without saying goodbye. I didn't mind. That had been a weepy "I love you, man" dialogue in comparison with a lot of our conversations.

Gloria returned to the living room. She set down plates holding buttered toast and fruit yogurt containers. She handed me a spoon.

"Who was that?"

I explained, emphasizing the significance of the bird being a coastal tanager.

"Hang on," I said, something occurring to me.

I walked into the bedroom and retrieved my wallet from where I'd jammed it in a shoe the night before during our disrobing. I dug out the card that Deanna Fleisher gave to me two mornings ago. The wildlife biologist who inadvertently saved my bacon at Mendon Woods. I returned to the living room and tapped out a message to her cell phone asking if she could call when she was free, and attached a picture of the bird. I told Gloria what I was up to.

She said, "So basically this bird is the connection between the two swamps."

"Looks like it."

"But why kill them up here?"

I thought back to the freezer full of birds. "The obvious conclusion is someone is trying to influence the lawsuit somehow," I said. "Fewer birds somehow tilts things in favor of developing Mendon Woods?"

"That makes sense, I guess. But then why freeze them?"

"To preserve them, like you said last night. But why bother? Why not just dump the bodies someplace?"

We ate for a couple of minutes without coming up with any easy explanation.

Finally, I said, "So what we know is someone appears to be offing rare birds from Heyder's Creek. The same bird that's the focus of a lawsuit about a swamp the judge is overseeing in Columbus."

"We went over that already—"

"Yeah. But it makes me wonder about something else."

"Like what?" Gloria said.

"Like Todd Orick."

"What about him?"

I was about to respond when another thought occurred to me. I pulled out my phone and scrolled through the photos. I stopped at the picture Todd's mother sent me from the photo roll on her iPad. I stood up and went to the refrigerator. I opened the freezer and retrieved the bird—the coastal tanager, we now knew—that we stored there last night. I set it on the kitchen table and propped my phone beside it. I swiped to enlarge the selfie of Todd in the swamp. Soon he was out of the frame, with the branch behind him enlarged. The branch and the bird sitting on it.

"Is that what I think it is?" Gloria said, looking over my shoulder.

"It's fuzzy. But it looks like one of these." I nodded at the bird on the plate. "Like I said, makes me wonder."

"And like I asked, about what?"

"If Todd saw something at Heyder's Creek he wasn't supposed to."

33

WE SAT IN SILENCE for a couple more minutes, crunching our toast, drinking our coffee, scratching the heads of Rottweilers, and considering the possibilities.

"That's a hell of a hypothesis," Gloria said at last.

"If it's true."

"What can we do to prove it?"

"Not sure, exactly. I guess I'll start by going to Cleveland. That's where the trail's leading. Maybe Randall P. Schiff can enlighten me."

"You're going now?"

"Once it's a little lighter."

"What about the law school connection?"

"I need to figure out how to approach that. Find someone who knew them both, someone I could pose some questions to without raising suspicion."

"Any prospects?"

"Unfortunately, yes."

"Unfortunately?"

"The one person I can think of is the last person who's going to want to talk."

"Who is it?"

"The judge's ex-husband."

I gave Gloria the Snapchat version of Paul and Laura's breakup. The lasting enmity on both sides—Laura at being jilted, Paul at the hostility of Laura's demands in the divorce settlement. The toll the split took on the kids—again, nothing I heard directly from Laura. But the facts were well known around the courthouse. Their daughter, Hannah, managed better, according to those in the know. She was now in school herself, at Kenyon College, not all that far from Homer. By contrast Laura's son—Dan? Dave?—fared worse in the aftermath, struggling to find himself. A Columbus State dropout for now, as far as I knew.

"Sounds par for the course, you ask me," Gloria said. "How well do you get on with your exes?"

"It's a mixed bag." Kym and I had reached a détente of sorts in recent years, united in the mission of trying to civilize a son who was at least as boisterous and ambitious as I'd been. By contrast, Joe's mom, Crystal, was someone I still wouldn't turn my back on in a room full of knives. It often felt like she and her husband, Bob, both party-hearty, happy-go-lucky types, didn't know what to do with quiet, introspective Joe, and so just didn't bother.

I said, "What about you?"

"Me?"

"You and your ex."

"Well, hard to avoid Al, being he's on the job with Mansfield city. Every so often we show up at the same scene. If that happens we talk, but we don't talk, if you know what I mean."

I told her I did.

"So how are you going to work it? With the judge's ex?"

"I'm not sure yet. Ideally I'd do it in person. But I don't want to lose momentum."

"I'd volunteer, but I need to stick around. I go on at noon, and after last night I want to keep an eye on things, see if anything changes. Plus, see if I can figure out who might have been coming up from Columbus, like that guy said. And if the powers-that-be suspect something's up." She picked up her own phone, sitting beside her plate on the dining room table, checked the time, and looked at me. "Add to that, my daughter's dropping the kids off in about an hour while she runs some errands."

"In that case, I better get going."

"Hayes."

"What?"

"You get concussed when you were playing?"

"A couple times, yeah."

"Affect your hearing?"

"I don't think so. Why?"

"Because I just said my daughter's dropping the kids off in about an hour."

"Yes, I heard you—"

"An hour, Hayes."

"An *hour*," I said, lightbulb coming on. "Why didn't you say so?"

"I just did."

"Yes, indeed," I said, setting my plate on the coffee table as she walked in my direction.

And so I ended up spending some time prone on Gloria's couch after all.

FORTY-FIVE MINUTES LATER, I was dressed, outside, and in my van at the back of the house. I started up the Odyssey and waited for Gloria to text me from just inside the door where she was watching the road.

All clear

Thanks

All business. It was all right. We each appreciated the other without question. But we also understood the stakes of what brought us together in the first place, and the greater need to find some answers, and soon.

I made my way back toward town, keeping a close eye out for suspicious vehicles and ticked-off raccoons. I saw nothing out of the ordinary. Traffic was what you'd expect on a weekday morning as people headed to jobs or early school starts.

In my rearview mirror I watched as the wind turbine on the ridge above the Oricks' house turned lazily, only a late summer breeze available to move the giant blades. It occurred to me that Todd's father never explained to me what was dangerous about it. No matter. Ten minutes later I was on the highway, headed for Cleveland.

34

AS I DROVE, I dealt possible scenarios in my mind for contacting Laura's ex-husband like solitaire cards, only to discard each in disgust.

"Hi, Paul. You don't know me, but I used to sleep with your ex-wife, and now she's missing."

"I'm sorry to bother you at the office. Any chance you, your ex-wife, and a guy named Randall P. Schiff were caught up in a love triangle two decades ago in law school?"

"Apologies for hitting you out of the blue with this, especially given the way you broke your ex's heart that morning at breakfast—"

I shook my head. I could do this all day and not get it right. I checked the time on the van's dashboard. Not quite nine. Hard to know if Paul would even be at his downtown firm in Columbus yet. I decided to find out.

"Paul Thayer's office," a female voice said after I penetrated the firm's defensive shields and was transferred back.

Given the circumstances, I decided against obfuscation. I identified myself by name and asked for Thayer. She informed me he wasn't in yet and would I care to leave a message. I waited for her to mention voice mail, to no avail. Old school. OK, then. I gave her my number and asked if he could return the call.

"May I let Mr. Thayer know why you're calling?"

"Tell him it's about Randall Schiff."

"Could you spell that, please?"

I did so.

"All right, Mr. Hayes, I'll let Mr. Thayer—"

"Randall Schiff, and Judge Laura Porter."

A pause. "Excuse me?"

"Tell Mr. Thayer it has to do with Randall Schiff and with Judge Porter."

Fifteen minutes later I pulled into a gas and convenience store complex on the edge of Ashland—"World Capital of Nice People," according to the sign at the exit. I'd have to fact-check that another day. After I filled up and replenished my coffee cup, I glanced at my e-mail and saw a new message from Bonnie. She was flagging something else about the sentencing of the woman who'd threatened the judge.

Check out the comments. Kind of interesting. If you're still working on something with that judge, I mean.

Squinting at my screen, I read the comments popping up below the article. They were about what you'd guess given the racial animosity surrounding the case. Supporting Laura were posts such as Long live the Velvet Fist and Anybody surprised a boy like that had a baby mama like her? Presumably referring to the woman's son—the beneficiary of the long sentence that led to the outburst.

Posts expressing outrage at the woman's treatment included comments such as First driving while black now talking like black??, an ironic #whitelivesmatter doncha get it?? and So much for the First Amendment. But it was a comment near the bottom that caught my attention.

That lady's just lucky she don't get blamed for messing with the judge's son too

The writer was someone named SouthSideMama99. Her icon was a generic silhouette. I tried to imagine what she was talking about. Had something happened to Laura's son? Dave? No. It came to me. *Daniel.* The college drop-out. Lived in Columbus but not with either parent, as far as I knew. Laura hadn't mentioned anything about him in our brief conversation in her car. I thought back to the call she received. The man whose caller ID photo I caught a glimpse of. Daniel? But if so, why hadn't she said anything? I realized I didn't even know his last name, Porter or Thayer. I tried Google searches with both, to no avail. Certainly nothing that resembled a news report of something bad—violence or an arrest. Strange.

There was no way to contact SouthSideMama99 directly, so I simply replied to her post, including my phone number.

This is interesting to me. Could you give me a call?

I waited a few minutes in hopes of receiving a response from her or a callback from Paul Thayer, but my phone stayed silent. It was all right. I had enough feelers out. It was just a matter of waiting to see which line bobbed in the water first.

Turns out, it didn't take long.

35

THE CALL CAME JUST minutes after I started back up the highway. Deanna Fleischer, the state wildlife biologist.

"The picture you sent me, that coastal tanager. Where's it from?"

I explained I was pretty certain it recently inhabited a wetland called Heyder's Creek near Mansfield. I left out the details leading to that discovery, including the barn, the freezer, and Gloria's and my suspicions that the birds were being preserved for nefarious purposes.

"That's a shame. That used to be a big stopover for them. I've heard there's barely any left up there."

I thought of all the specimens I spied in the freezer.

"So what can you tell me about them?"

"They're a pretty special bird."

"Special how?"

She related an abbreviated version of the coastal tanager's bio. Native to Piauí State on the northeastern coast of Brazil. Treasured for their unique, trilling song and Cleveland Browns-like plumage. Reliant on category III North American wetlands such as Mendon Woods and Heyder's Creek: after traveling thousands of miles north each spring, the birds needed the refuge these niche environments provided. For whatever reason, coastal tanagers were also more susceptible to changes in their sur-roundings than other avian species. A combination of modern farming practices that plowed under hedgerows, the increased use of pesticides, and the disappearance of wetlands was causing their numbers to plummet.

I said, "Doesn't sound good. It may explain—"

"Oh, and wind turbines."

"What?"

"There's been quite a few killed flying into turbine blades."

"In Ohio?"

"Some here. A lot in Illinois."

I recalled the machine on the ridge above Todd Orick's par-ents' house, blades slowly turning in the late summer breeze. The way it dominated the landscape for miles around. The un-happiness of people over the prospect of more—the impact on tourism in places like Mohican and Richland Counties. And what Todd's father said. *Still wish to hell they'd get rid of it . . . Dangerous, that's why.* Was this the danger he was talking about? To birds?

I told Fleischman what I was thinking.

"There might have been some kills up there, by Mansfield. I can check. But the thing is—"

"Yes?"

"You never told me exactly what your interest in all this is. The bird, and Mendon Woods. What you were doing out there the other morning to begin with. And that guy. I did you a real favor, you know, not calling the police."

"I know. But the thing is, it's complicated, and—"

"Sounds like it. But if you're representing the developer, we're done talking. I'm on the other side. Plus, you can imagine how I feel about losing that swamp, given the pressure on this bird."

"I'm not involved in the lawsuit." It was an off-white lie, but I soldiered on, afraid to lose this opportunity. "I'm interested in coastal tanagers for another reason. My question for you is trying to understand these migration patterns."

"What reason?" Her voice was tinged with suspicion. Who could blame her?

"I can't divulge that right now."

"Then why should I talk to you?"

"You should talk to me because there's something strange about this lawsuit—"

"I thought you said you weren't—"

"I'm not. But I know some things that might connect with things I don't understand. Yet."

"That's ridiculous. Either you are or you aren't involved."

"I know how it sounds. But just hear me out. This development—do we even know what it is?"

"Not really. Commercially zoned is what they want, but that's one of the frustrating aspects about it. It's like this big secret."

"OK." That was consistent with what Bonnie found. "And Mendon Woods—what happens to the coastal tanager if the developer wins?"

"I can't really—"

"I'm not asking you to take a legal position, or even comment on the lawsuit. But professionally speaking. As a biologist. As a"—I struggled for the right phrase, realizing how much hung on the wording—"as an advocate for the bird."

A long pause. So long I was afraid she disconnected. I slowed to sixty to let traffic move over, trucks headed for the cloverleaf I-76 exit toward Akron.

"It's not that simple a question."

"Why not?"

"You said you were familiar with the lawsuit?"

"For the most part."

"In that case, you know it isn't really about the wetlands. I mean, it is, of course. But that's not what the judge is deciding. Judge Porter?"

"That's right. She's not?"

"Not directly. The lawsuit is really about the bird. The judge is being asked to rule on the impact of the loss of Mendon Woods on the coastal tanager, and whether one of these drainage ditch replacements is good enough."

"Is it?"

A derisive laugh. "Not by a long shot. It's a joke. It's like trading an old-growth forest for a Christmas tree farm."

"Isn't it cut and dried, then? Pave over Mendon Woods and you lose another coastal tanager habitat?"

"Yeah. But she has to keep in mind the domino effect."

"Meaning?"

"This bird's disappearing anyway. Ohio's just a small part of the equation. It's a problem that reaches all the way back to Brazil. Now there's a country that knows something about getting rid of natural areas. So the question is whether a swamp in Columbus would make any difference at this point."

"I see. So what would help her make that decision?"

"A lot of things, starting with the outlook for the bird. If the population is hanging in there, and Mendon Woods is part of a survival strategy, there's a strong argument for keeping the swamp as is. But if the coastal tanager is essentially extinct in the state, the argument's going to be, well, what difference would a dinky wetland make at this point?"

I thought about this. "Heyder's Creek. The other place where they're known to summer."

"What about it?"

"If there were still a lot of birds in and around Heyder's Creek, that's good for Mendon Woods. For your side."

"That's right."

"But if the bird is also disappearing from there—or maybe gone, even—it helps the Columbus developer."

"I'm afraid so. Because it means the dominos have fallen. And I'm worried, because of that picture you sent me. If the birds are dying up there, that's the end."

"The end?"

"The end of the coastal tanager. No birds in Heyder's Creek makes it hard not to draw a line through Mendon Woods. And if the judge does that, they'll be gone from North America—maybe gone for good—in less than five years. But don't worry."

"Why not?"

"There'll still be plenty of websites where you can see a really nice picture of it. Right next to the passenger pigeon and the dodo bird."

36

SHE HUNG UP AFTER another minute, sounding disconsolate. I couldn't blame her. I'd just given her reason to believe a cause she devoted a lot of energy to, probably a good portion of her career, was lost. Our conversation didn't explain the trouble the judge was in. But it went a long way toward illuminating the stakes at play in the lawsuit over the Columbus swamp, whatever this commercial zoning was for. Keeping an eye on the road, I pressed redial for Gloria's number. I heard her recorded voice tell me in no-nonsense terms to leave her a message. I went over my conversation with the biologist, and drew her attention to the wind-turbine kills. I asked if any had been discovered in Mohican Township, and to call me as soon as she knew anything.

Not even a minute later my phone rang again. That was fast. But when I answered it was someone else altogether.

"Who is this?" A woman's voice.

I told her my name and asked who was calling. Instead of answering, she said, "Why'd you tell me to call?"

"Did I?"

"You sent me a message. On the internet. On that story."

It came back to me. SouthSideMama99. Her message after the article about the community service sentence for the woman who threatened Laura. *That lady's just lucky she don't get blamed for messing with the judge's son too*

"Right. Sorry to be confused. I was interested in what you wrote."

"Why?"

"It might be related to something I'm working on. A case."

"A case? You a cop?"

I paused as I slowed, traffic backing up ahead of me now that I was in the Cleveland metro area. I passed the Ford plant in Brook Park, clouds of steam rising from a welter of pipes on the factory rooftops to my left. I explained who I was and why I contacted her. At last she agreed to answer questions if she could.

"So what did you mean, about the judge's son?"

"Maybe I shouldn't have written that. You know?"

"Why not?"

"All I know is what my daughter told me. OK? I don't want no trouble."

"Me neither. What did she tell you?"

"She just told me what Charlie told her."

"Who's Charlie?"

"Her boyfriend."

"Does he know the judge's son?"

"Not exactly."

"What then?"

"It's because of his job."

Patiently, I said, "His job?"

"He's a locksmith. Apprentice. Finally found something he's good at, thank you Jesus. Missy's real happy about it."

"That's your daughter?"

"Yeah. She and Charlie are having a baby. So she's feeling good he's got a job. She was starting to wonder. Yeah, I was wondering too. Last place he worked he lasted two weeks and—"

"He knows the judge's son because of his job?"

"What I said."

"How?"

"How what?"

"How does his job relate to knowing the judge's son?" I was beginning to wonder if I might end up in Lake Erie before she got to the point.

"So Charlie gets a call to go change locks at this house off Summit. Fourteenth, Fifteenth Street, somewhere in there."

"OK." I knew the area slightly. North of campus, three-story brick piles, on the edge of some gentrification but rough around the edges. "So what happened?"

"Well, the guy had a break-in. Wanted new locks, front and back."

"A burglary?"

"Not exactly."

"Meaning what?"

"I'm just telling you what Missy told me that Charlie told her, OK?"

"OK," I said, suppressing a sigh.

"So, meaning that the kid—this judge's son—come into his apartment one day, goes into the kitchen, and freaks out."

"Why?"

"There's a dead bird on the table."

My heart sped up. "A bird?"

"That's what Missy said. A bird, and a note."

"A note?"

"You heard me. The bird had a note tied to its neck."

"What did it say?"

"*Accidents happen.*"

ON THE SPUR OF the moment I took the exit at 150th Street and left the highway. This was no longer a conversation I wanted to have while driving. I turned left, gauged my options, and saw a diner called Somer's up ahead, the "o" in "Somer's" a bright sun. Why not. I pulled into the parking lot.

"Hang on," I said. "How did Charlie know who this kid was? That he was the son of that judge?"

"Because he paid with her credit card. Charlie told the kid it would be better if she did it herself, either in person or on the phone. But the kid explained she was a judge and wasn't around just then. Charlie told Missy and Missy looked her up."

Accidents happen.

"When was this?"

She thought about it, and then reported it was Monday. Late afternoon.

After Laura called and asked to see me. But before she got the phone call that stopped everything in its tracks. *My God—are you all right?* I tried again to picture the photo that popped up on her caller ID.

"Any idea what kind of bird?"

"Charlie didn't say."

"Was there a police report?"

"About what?"

"About this break-in, or the bird, or whatever?"

"I don't think so. They're supposed to ask, in case there's insurance involved or something. But the kid—the judge's son?"

"Daniel."

"Yeah. He said the police weren't involved. He said he and his mom just wanted the locks changed to make sure nobody could get in again. Said the landlord agreed to it, so that was that."

We talked for another couple minutes. I pressed her for any details she might have left out. There wasn't much more. She confirmed Daniel's last name was Thayer. She told me her name, Shoshanna, and said she wasn't exactly sure why she posted the comment except she kind of felt for the lady who got sentenced, even though she herself was white, you know? She asked if she was in trouble. I told her no. I also told her to call me if Charlie had any additional contact with Daniel. She said that she would, though her tone suggested otherwise.

After I disconnected, I went into the restaurant and ordered a cup of coffee to go. While I waited I thought about the implications of the call. Laura was overseeing a lawsuit dependent on the fate of a rare bird. Out of the blue, someone delivers the body of said species *Godfather*-horse-head style not to her, but to her son. But why? Sending a message that would really count? It seemed a harsh, over-the-top maneuver. The kind of thing you'd do as a last resort. A message following—

I was interrupted by my phone going off. Gloria calling. I answered as the checkout counter lady returned with my coffee. I juggled the phone and my wallet as I paid her and nodded my thanks.

"Hayes," Gloria said. "That biologist lady was right. There've been three documented bird kills at that turbine in the last three months. Masses of them. And a bunch were coastal tanagers."

37

I WALKED BACK TO my van and leaned against the driver's side door, holding my coffee. I listened while Gloria explained what she found on the internet and from calling some people at the sheriff's department she trusted. I heard the babble of children's voices in the background.

"So these birds are flying into the turbine blades?" I asked.

"That's what the reports say. But there's a couple weird things about it."

"Like what?"

"For one, I guess these coastal tanager guys aren't really a flock bird. But with these kills? They always find a bunch together. Add to that, the bodies show up in the morning, like they were flying around at night and got hit."

"Let me guess. They're not nocturnal."

"Not as far as anybody knows. I'll tell you this, the kills aren't doing the turbine company any favors. People are pissed, saying it's exactly what they worried about."

I recalled Dave Orick's explanation of opposition to the turbine on the grounds it was bad for tourism. Between bird kills and ruining the vista, this was not a popular machine.

"So they're not nocturnal, and they don't fly in flocks. But a bunch were found dead each time."

"That's right. Mixed in with others, robins and sparrows. Same as what you found in the freezer."

"Necks broken?"

"That's what I was told. Like that one you grabbed."

"So maybe they're not really dying by hitting the turbine."

"What I'm thinking. We wondered why anyone would freeze a bunch of birds, right? Maybe that's why."

"Idea being, someone caught and killed all these birds a while ago, but they're dumping them gradually, to make it look more natural."

"It's a possibility," Gloria said.

"And maybe—"

"What?"

"Maybe that's what Todd Orick saw, that he wasn't supposed to."

"What do you mean?"

"Maybe he saw somebody catching these birds, that morning he was in the swamp fishing. And whoever it was had to make sure there were no witnesses."

We didn't say anything as we considered the possibility. I pulled the plastic lid off my Styrofoam cup, blew on the coffee, and took a sip. Thought about the look in Tear Drop's eyes as he came at me with the knife at Mendon Woods. I told Gloria what Shoshanna—SouthSideMama99—related about the judge's son and the dead bird in his kitchen.

"OK, that's really freaky."

"No shit. But the question now is, was that a one-off or part of a pattern?"

"I don't follow."

I said, "We know this lawsuit over Mendon Woods is high-pressure, right?"

"Sure, according to everything you've told me."

"So there's a lot at stake. But it's also a different angle on environmental preservation." I went over the wildlife biologist's explanation of the declining coastal tanager population and the domino effect. "The judge is already taking heat from both sides on the ruling. Why target her son like that, out of the blue?"

"Easy. It sends a scary fucking message."

"A message, or an ultimatum?"

"What's the difference?" Gloria said.

"The difference is whether someone already warned the judge she had to rule against the bird, or else."

"Or else what?"

"Or else I have no idea. But the point is, maybe she didn't listen. Told them no. So they up the ante."

"By threatening her son."

"That's right," I said.

"But why not go to the police? Why go to you instead? No offense. Other than your history with her."

"I can't answer that. There must be a reason she feels she can't. That's a question I'm hoping either her ex-husband or Randall P. Schiff can answer."

"So what are you going to do now?"

"I guess I'll pay Schiff a visit at his office. See what he can tell me."

"You think that's a good idea?"

"No clue. But it's the only one I've got right now."

"All right. Be careful. OK, Hayes?"

"I'll do my best."

I cut the connection and plugged the directions for Schiff's firm into my phone. I was about to drive out of the restaurant parking lot when I decided to try Paul Thayer again. Shoshanna's story of the dead bird in the apartment made me all the more eager to learn what I could about Schiff and his connections to the judge, however long ago they were.

I went through the same routine with the firm's receptionist and the transfer back to Thayer's office. This time his secretary told me to please hold a moment. A couple of seconds later I heard a brusque male voice.

"Paul Thayer."

"It's Andy Hayes. I called earlier. I wanted—"

"I know you called. The question is what the hell you're up to."

38

I TOOK A DEEP breath. It occurred to me I was talking to the person who inadvertently got me into this entire mess. Had he not had his affair and divorced the judge, she and I would never have connected to begin with. Likewise, she wouldn't have sought me out when her problems arose—whatever they were, exactly.

I said, "I'm not up to anything. I just need to ask you a couple of questions."

"About Randy Schiff and my ex-wife? Is this some kind of joke? I know who you are, all right? If you think—"

"If I think what?"

Could Thayer know about Laura's and my past? It seemed unlikely, given the care we'd taken—that Laura had taken—to keep our relationship a secret. But I also knew secrets were hard to cover up forever.

"A private eye with your reputation, digging up two-decade-old dirt? That's low, even for you. But let me guess, you're working for O'Malley. So let me make one thing clear—"

O'Malley—the judge running against Laura for the Supreme Court seat.

"I'm not working for Judge O'Malley."

"Give me a break. Do you think I was born—"

"I said I'm not working for him."

"Who then?"

I took another breath. "I'm working for Laura."

I looked up the street, watched the traffic passing on the elevated lanes of I-71. Felt dread in the pit of my stomach as I thought about Shoshanna's story of the dead bird on Daniel's kitchen table and my growing fears about the judge, fears compounded by the idea that time was running out. The morning was growing late and I had yet to make it anywhere near Schiff.

"For Laura," her ex-husband said.

"That's right."

"As what? Bodyguard?" The sneer loud and clear, even over the phone.

"I can't tell you."

"Jesus. That's convenient."

"But to repeat, it has nothing to do with Judge O'Malley."

"Then what? Why could you possibly be interested in Laura and Randy if you're not—"

"What if I told you I was really interested in the Berman Prize?"

A pause. "The Berman Prize? What the hell does that have to do with anything?"

"I don't know. But just give me five minutes. This conversation can be off the record or privileged or pinky-swear secret or whatever you want. I'll explain everything as soon as I can. I promise."

"But why—"

"Five minutes."

"Three. I've got a deposition to get to. And you can promise anything you want, but it doesn't mean I'm answering a single question."

"Then all I can do is ask. So—the Berman Prize."

"What about it?"

"Laura won it. Used it to go through law school."

"Public knowledge," Thayer said impatiently. "You can look up the winners on the school website. If that's all—"

"Did Randy Schiff win it too?"

"No—of course not."

"Somebody else then, besides Laura?"

"Do your research. It's one per class. It has to be. It's a lot of money. It pays for everything."

"Did Schiff apply?"

"I'm not sure. Two minutes."

"Not sure—so he could have?"

"He might have, as I recall."

"OK. During law school, were he and Laura an item?"

"Oh, here we go. Back to the dirt."

"I'm not looking for dirt. It's a simple question."

"Why should I answer it?"

"Because it could help Laura."

"Help her how?"

"I told you, I can't tell you yet."

A deep sigh. "Like this is what I need to be spending my time on this morning. Getting grilled by a washed-up ballplayer who won't tell me what he's up to."

"If you don't mind, I prefer successfully paroled. Could you please just help me out? Randy and Laura?"

"What about them?"

"Did they date in law school?"

"Yes. Satisfied? I don't see—"

"Before she met you?"

"Obviously."

"Did she break up with Randy to date you?"

"All right. That's it. I'm not going to—"

"Please. I know it's intrusive."

"Damn right it's intrusive. But I guess that's what you do, isn't it?"

I didn't say anything. He had no reason to talk to me and we both knew it. That's why his next words surprised me.

"Laura left Randy to be with me. All right?"

"Thanks—I really appreciate it."

"I bet you do. Now if you don't—"

"Did she and Randy stay friends? Afterward?"

Another pause. "Yes and no."

"Meaning?"

An even longer pause. "They—reconciled, I guess you could call it. Agreed to speak civilly to each other."

"Any idea why?"

"Why what?"

"Why they let bygones be bygones, or whatever."

"We—they had no choice." A change in his tone. Almost as if he were warming to the topic. "Law school was a hothouse, and we saw each other a lot. It was more efficient to just bury the hatchet. They used to—"

"Used to what?"

"Used to study together. He offered to help her with papers, things like that."

"Did that bother you?"

"No," he said, unconvincingly. "Laura sometimes overextended herself. Ran up against last-minute deadlines, and needed extra help. You've got one minute."

"Do you have any idea why Laura would be back in touch with Randy now?"

"None, other than the obvious."

"The obvious?"

"They're restarting things. Good for them, if it's true. But I don't know, nor do I care. We're not married anymore, so it's none of my business."

"Do you have any idea why Laura would have reason to be"—I hesitated, weighing the word I wanted to use—"would have regrets about winning the Berman Prize?" I pictured the smashed frame in the wastepaper basket.

"That's actually the dumbest thing you've asked so far. Why would she? It's the most prestigious scholarship at the school. It was tough to win and almost as tough to hang onto."

"Hang onto? Why?"

"Again, do your homework. Tough because the requirements were so rigorous. GPA and all that, and the public service requirement. But she couldn't have regretted it because it got her through school, and frankly, it launched her career, after the DOJ stint. And that led to—"

I waited. He didn't continue. He didn't have to. One thing led to another, and that's why they weren't married anymore.

Thayer said, "So what in the hell is all this about, now that I've dug up a bunch of ancient history for you against my better judgment?"

"When was the last time you talked to Laura?"

"I have no idea. Months. We communicate via e-mail about our daughter's tuition. That's it."

"And Randy Schiff?"

"Not since the day we walked out of the bar exam. Answer my question."

I thought about his son and the bird on the table. Should I mention that? To what end? Why open that can of worms, when I wasn't ready to reveal the far more serious issue of his ex-wife possibly being in danger?

"I can't. Like I said, I'm going to keep my promise and fill you in eventually. But I need to hang up and figure some things out. I'm sorry to have troubled you. It's important. That's all I can tell you."

"Then here's what I can tell *you*. If I see anything in the news, anything about any of this that looks like O'Malley planted it, I'm coming down on you as hard as I can. I know people at the Department of Public Safety. Your license won't be worth shit when I'm done."

"You won't have to do that because you're not going to see anything because I'm not working for William O'Malley."

"How can I be sure?"

"You can be sure because I told you I'm not," I said, and bid him goodbye.

39

DESPITE THE TIME I was losing, I had at least one more call to make to ease my conscience, based on what South-SideMama99 told me. Still standing in the parking lot of Somers Restaurant, I called Otto Mulligan. He answered on the third ring.

"Woody?" he said.

"You have a second?"

"Not really. I'm in the middle of something."

"You available later? I might have a job for you."

"Where?"

"In Columbus."

"Sorry, Woody. I'm out of town."

Mulligan was on a short—a very short—list of people I permitted use of my old nickname. The one I received in high school that stuck seemingly forever. Andy "Woody" Hayes. The nickname two ex-wives and an ex-fiancée once knew me by, and yes, with the curtains drawn and our clothes off, they all made the same off-color joke. The nickname most people believed paid homage to legendary Ohio State coach Woody Hayes. Which it did in a way, but not how people imagined. Hayes was fired in 1978 for punching a Clemson player near the end of the Gator Bowl. I took his nickname a decade or so later when I punched an opposing player in a state semifinal game after the guy made one too many racial slurs about a black teammate of mine. And so legends are created, and misconstrued.

I said, "Where are you?"

"Ashland."

"Ashland?" The small Ohio city where I stopped for gas earlier that day. "What are you doing there?"

"Got a bead on a domestic violence perp I've been looking for. I'm told he slunk up here to hide out at Grandma's. I'm over the river, and I'm going through the woods now."

"I thought Ashland was the world capital of nice people."

"All except this guy, Woody."

Mulligan was a bail bondsman with an office across from the courthouse. He was also my go-to muscleman, partly because he was damn good at his job and partly because he can carry a weapon and I can't, thanks to my conviction.

"So what's going on?" he said.

"I need a wellness check. On the son of a client."

"Big Dog's up here with me. But Buck might be available."

"I'll get back to you on that, thanks." Mulligan's hired help, though competent, could be a little scary, and I didn't want to add stress to Laura's son at this point.

"I hear you. Buck's not always ready for prime time. How about Theresa?"

"Theresa?"

"Why not? She's at least as tough as me, and a hell of a lot prettier. And we're talking checkup, right, not a firefight?"

"As far as I know. Actually, that's a pretty good idea."

"On the house, Woody. Listen, gotta run. I'll let you know when I'm back in town. We'll get together and lift a few."

"I thought you didn't drink."

"Lift *weights*, Woody. Get your head on straight."

"That may take some doing," I said, and disconnected. I thought about his suggestion, looked at it a couple different ways, and failed to find any holes in it. I punched in the number. Theresa Sullivan also answered on the third ring.

"What now, QB?"

"I've got a little job for you, if you're—"

"I'm glad you called. I've got a good one for you. There's this—"

"I don't really have time, Theresa. If you could just—"

"Where's the fire, QB? Anyway, there's this football player, and he goes to the library, and he tells the librarian he has to read a play by Shakespeare."

"Theresa—"

"Librarian says to him, 'Which one?' Want to know what he says?"

"Do I have a choice?"

"The player shrugs and says, 'William, I guess.' Get it?"

"I get it."

Theresa Sullivan loved nothing more than peppering me with dumb football player jokes. She did it to get under my skin, but also to remind me she knew a few players herself in the day, and how smart could a jock be anyway if he was looking for action on the streets of Columbus with a prostitute instead of trolling the campus bars? But sure enough it happened, and she had the calluses on her knees to prove it. That was long ago now, in the days before she left the streets and became an outreach worker to trafficked women trying to escape the same life.

Before she had time to conjure up another joke, I explained why I was calling.

"Just check on the guy?"

"Just see if he's all right. Explain you're a friend of mine, and that I'm a friend of his mother's. Work it however you want. I just want—"

"Want what?"

"I just want to be sure he's OK. It'll make what I'm doing up here easier."

"Which is what?"

"It would take a while to explain. But you're doing me a big favor. No, more than a favor—it's a paying gig."

"How much?" she demanded.

I thought for a second. "Hundred bucks."

"That could buy a lot of shampoo."

Theresa worked for an Episcopal church in the poor neighborhood west of downtown dubbed the Bottoms. One of the church's outreach efforts included expeditions where she and several volunteers handed out toiletries to girls and women on the street, to help them out but also to provide an entrée to get them to talk to Theresa about trying to leave the life.

"That it could. Or you could also spend it on yourself."

"I may just split the difference, QB. I got my eye on a new bracelet at Red Giraffe. All right. I'll do it. Just send me the details."

"Thanks."

"Hundred bucks—don't forget."

I told her I wouldn't, disconnected, pocketed my phone, and climbed into my van. She'd be fine, I told myself. For my part I needed to be moving. I needed to focus on the task at hand. It was time to return to Cleveland—and track down Randall P. Schiff.

40

FIFTEEN MINUTES LATER I was driving across the elevated bridge where I-71 ends and I-90 picks up. I looked at the Cleveland skyline growing bigger the closer I neared. I put on my signal for the East Ninth Street exit and moved into the right lane.

Even today, with all the changes the city has undergone, the skyline was still dominated by the Terminal Tower, a soaring Art Deco middle finger to the naysayers of the world who ever doubted the city's ability to survive. Closer in stood Progressive Field, the home of the Indians, who over the years reversed fortunes with the Browns, who in my day—as my dad observed—actually won a few games, while the Tribe were rarely out of the basement of the standings. Talk about a 180-degree turn for both teams. Browns Stadium was on the far side of downtown, on the lake, and so out of view for now. Just as well. I might or might not swing by. For just a second I heard first the roar of a crowd in my mind, then an increasingly loud rumble of boos. No matter how much I wish it were lower down on my Wikipedia page, it's always near the top: *Hayes also holds the Cleveland Browns franchise record for most interceptions in a single game: five, on the last day he ever took the field.*

Exiting off the highway, pangs of regret washed over me like the ritual dumping of a Gatorade bucket I never received up here. After my senior-year debacle at Ohio State and the criminal conviction that followed, I'd been given a second chance in the NFL and proceeded to shit all over it. True to form, I spent the night before that record-setting last game barhopping with a woman through the west-side suburb of Lakewood before ending up back in her apartment, which featured an authentic *A Christmas Story* leg lamp in the living room. I awakened in her bed the next morning around the time I should have been checking into the locker room, the pounding in my head as if the linemen's sacks had already begun. Afterward, I couldn't get out of town fast enough.

And yet.

More than once I rued the lost chance to set down roots here. In my limited time in the city, I learned to appreciate Cleveland's brassy attitude, Old World ethnic diversity, and blue-collar work ethic, not to mention all those pierogi. Living here would also have provided a welcome break from the fanaticism of Ohio State fans in Columbus who couldn't forgive me for two-decade-old sins no matter how much time passed. Browns fans could be just as rough in the moment, but they had more experience with heartbreak and so tended to let bygones be bygones after a blue streak or two. I likened it to the difference in how certain married couples settled disagreements: the shout-it-out-and-move-on mentality of hot-blooded eastern European types, compared to the sit-and-sulk vibe of morose midwesterners.

But moving here would never happen. I owed it to my sons, if no one else, to take my medicine and stick around central Ohio. Spouses strayed, workers faked injuries, and witnesses held clues to crimes in Columbus as often as anyplace else, and increasingly, as the population climbed, more so.

I shook my head. It had been a charming walk down memory lane. My personal stroll of shame. But it was time to assemble my game face. I had to figure out the best approach to Schiff, I had to do it fast, and I had to be sure I didn't put Laura in danger—or more danger than she was already in.

DRIVING UP EAST NINTH past the Erie Street Cemetery, I reviewed what I knew at this point about the man I was on the way to confront. He and Laura both competed for the most prestigious scholarship at Ohio State's law school, with Laura coming out on top. Did Laura know he failed to win the Berman Prize, that she triumphed at his expense? My guess was yes, in part because they dated at some point after matriculating. Pillow talk was pillow talk, no matter how competitive.

Later, Laura broke up with Schiff to go out with Paul Thayer, who she would one day marry. She and Schiff remained friends of sorts. Study buddies. Along the way, she kept up her GPA and landed a summer job at the DOJ in Washington, a feather in her cap but necessary too, since she needed that component to keep the scholarship. That stint led her back to the U.S. Attorney's Office in Columbus, where her work as a federal prosecutor helped launch her political career. I reminded myself of the call I needed to make to my contact in that office. An AUSA named Pete Henderson, renowned for his ability not to hang up on me straightaway.

Fast-forward a couple of decades. Schiff, a lawyer in his hometown of Cleveland, contributes generously to Laura's Supreme Court campaign. First on his own, then through PG Inc., a cloud-computing company tied to a rising European AI firm. Those companies were connected to a developer interested in a wetland whose fate Laura held in her hands. The obvious conclusion: Schiff had his own interest in the swamp, or at least the hundreds of acres surrounding it. I recalled Flota's unsuccessful efforts to launch a project in Indiana. If not there, next stop Ohio? Was the failure to launch in Indiana the reason for the secrecy about the project in Columbus?

Then, as the Mendon Woods lawsuit wound down, someone delivers Laura's son an ominous warning. *Accidents happen.*

A warning which implies Laura has ignored a request—a demand?—to rule against the coastal tanager and give the developer the victory. In the meantime, I'm attacked during an innocent nature hike through Mendon Woods, meaning someone has connected me to Laura. The person who attacked me—my old pal Tear Drop—has part of Schiff's business card with him outside a barn holding a freezer filled with dead birds. And who were Tear Drop and friend expecting from Columbus that night?

Question one: Were Schiff and Tear Drop connected? Almost certainly, it seemed to me. But how? Whatever else you might say about my attacker, he didn't seem the law school type. I thought idly of the apartment complex Schiff owned. A connection there? Anything was possible at this point, I supposed.

Question two: Was Schiff the one putting pressure on Laura to rule against the coastal tanager? Less certainly, but circumstantial evidence said yes. Again, why the secrecy?

Question three: As all this was happening, why would Laura trash the certificate of the Berman Prize, one of her greatest early accomplishments? Was she now ashamed of it for some reason? Was that shame connected to a renewed acquaintanceship with her former lover and ex-classmate Randall P. Schiff?

I thought again of the summer Laura spent with the DOJ. In all the time we were together, it was the one experience she shared with me, if you count five minutes recalling her thrill at walking those corridors and working on, as she put it, "Cases that really mattered." Her equivalent of a schoolgirl gushing over a cool field trip. Translation: it was a summer that meant a lot to her, and not just because it allowed her to keep her scholarship. Although that had to be always on her mind. Then there was the line you could draw from that experience straight to her campaign for the highest court in Ohio.

Lots of questions. But no answers that added up to much of anything yet.

I pulled into a parking garage off Chester just south of Superior, drove up two levels, and squeezed my van between an

Escalade and a Mini Cooper. I lifted my phone off the passenger seat and scrolled through my contacts. Time for one more call. I found Pete Henderson of the U.S. Attorney's Office right where I left him, retrieved his number, and pressed the green send button.

41

HENDERSON'S PHONE RANG SO long I figured it would go to voice mail. But on the ninth or tenth ring he answered. I identified myself and asked, "Got a second?"

"Depends why you're calling."

"Would you believe a hot tip on the ponies?"

"Knowing you I would. What's up?"

"I have a favor to ask."

"If I can."

"That's my line. Let me rephrase. I'm calling a favor in."

Henderson worked violent crime and terrorism cases for the Southern District of Ohio, mostly in central Ohio. He was ex-FBI, played hard in a YMCA men's basketball league three times a week, and was married to his high school sweetheart, an elementary school teacher, which was kind of obnoxious, in my opinion. A few years back our paths intersected thanks to a mutual interest in a drug-and-guns gang called the Fourth Street Posse. More recently, he prosecuted the mother of the white supremacist who tried taking out half of downtown during Red, White & Boom, a woman I delivered more or less in a box tied with shiny ribbons. He was a nice enough guy, unless you had a thing for committing felonies. I told him I had a question involving Judge Laura Porter.

"The Velvet Fist, huh? What do you need to know?"

"For starters, I'm wondering if you worked together."

"We overlapped a year or two."

"There on Marconi?"

"The office was on North High, then. Two Nationwide Plaza. So what's going on?"

"I'm helping her out. Doing a little backgrounding."

"Is this about the campaign?"

"Tangentially, yes."

"Speak English. You're helping get her elected?"

I thought of the dollar I coaxed from Laura that night in her car.

"I'm working for her, but not on the campaign side."

"Good thing, since we're an apolitical office, as of course you know. I can't get involved in anything—"

"Like the appointment of U.S. attorneys has nothing to do with politics. Give me a break."

"That's the big boss. We're just worker bees at my level. Sworn to uphold the Constitution regardless of who's in office."

"Spare me the lecture. I'm not asking you to phone bank. I just need to know something."

"Like what?"

I explained about the Berman Prize. He'd heard of it, but that was about it. I reminded him of the public service component, in Laura's case the DOJ job, and the path it paved to the U.S. Attorney's Office and then to her first campaign.

"Her bio's common knowledge," Henderson said when I finished. "It might even be on her campaign website—not that I've been checking it out or anything. What's your interest?"

"How would you land an internship like that? With the DOJ?"

"Hell if I know. Maybe the dean pulled some strings."

"Maybe? Or for sure?"

"I have no idea. I didn't know her that well."

"Can you find out?"

"Find out what?"

"Can you find out how someone goes about landing a top-notch internship at the Justice Department to fulfill a requirement for a prestigious law school fellowship?"

"Oh yeah, no problem. Soon as I indict D. B. Cooper. Can't you just call the school yourself?"

"I'm backgrounding, remember? Trying to keep it on the QT."

"Backgrounding, but not for the campaign."

"That's right."

"That doesn't make any sense."

"I won't argue the point."

"So how does the Berman Prize pertain to anything—"

"I'm asking for a favor here, Pete. Just a call or two."

He didn't say anything for a moment. I heard a sound in the background, and realized it was a door closing. He came back on the line a second later.

"Listen closely, Andy. You were right about my boss. He's a Democrat with a big blue D on his forehead. He's got a wall filled with pictures of him and the Clintons and the Obamas and the Bidens—donkeys galore."

"Now who's telling me something I already know?"

He lowered his voice. "By contrast, Laura Porter is a Republican. Which is the opposite party, in case your detective skills are rusty. She's a damned good judge, just like she was a damned good prosecutor. And she'll make just as good a Supreme Court justice if she's elected. Extremely off the record, the chances I'll vote for her are high. But, back to my speech about worker bees, it wouldn't be cool for me to be caught doing anything that helps her out. Anything that contains the slightest whiff of campaigning. You understand where I'm coming from?"

"Loud and clear. And you're going to have to trust me when I say this has nothing to do with politics. I just don't know who else to call. I need to know about this internship. That's all."

"Bullshit."

"I'm sorry?"

"You heard me. I'm calling BS on this whole conversation. I know you too well. I'm guessing there's an entire below-the-surface iceberg of shit you're not telling me. A shitberg, we'll call it. I'm going to go out on a limb and predict that in a relatively short period of time, I'll be reading your name in the newspaper and saying—but not so my kids can hear—'What the fuck?' Because when you call, it means trouble—"

"Listen, Pete—"

"But fortunately for you, trouble tends to interest me. Occupational hazard and all. So I'll make some inquiries. If—"

"If?"

"If you promise to call me if there's an opportunity in whatever you're working on and not telling me about for my boss to stand up in front of some cameras and make a little hay."

"It's possible that could be arranged."

"Possible?"

"Highly probable."

"Right answer," Henderson said, and hung up without saying goodbye.

42

WALKING OUT OF THE garage, I plotted my approach to meeting Schiff. For starters, I had to assume he knew who I was. Someone or something alerted Tear Drop to my presence at Mendon Woods two mornings ago. Either he followed Laura to my house the night before, or spied me going back to her condo the next day, or some combination of the two. But the assault wasn't random. The fragment of Schiff's business card that Gloria found in the van just before she slipped it into neutral was the connecting factor, since there was also no question it was Tear Drop in the barn last night as I crouched behind the tractor wheel. So my standard ruse for weaseling into an office like Schiff's—lost pizza delivery guy—wasn't going to cut it. And not just because I can't stand wearing monogrammed golf shirts.

On the other hand, Schiff didn't necessarily have the whole picture about me. He didn't know my history with Laura—I could bank on that, if nothing else. Thanks to Gloria's ruse which allowed me to escape the barn undetected, he didn't know that I knew about the freezer full of birds and the dumping of dead coastal tanagers by the wind turbine. An act that disguised the fact someone—Tear Drop and friend?—were culling them from Heyder's Creek as part of a plan to influence the judge's decision on a swamp sixty miles south in Columbus. And he didn't know I knew about the bird that ended up on the kitchen table of Laura's son. That had been the luckiest break of all.

On the other hand, there were barns full of information about what was going on that I didn't know. Which more or less leveled the playing field, as far as I could see. I'd take the odds. I'd played on a few real fields that weren't level.

RAABE, KARABINUS, NORTHCOTT, RICKARD and Dowd took up three floors of a gleaming thirty-story office tower on Euclid around the corner from Playhouse Square. Walking there from the garage required maneuvering my way past cordons of orange barrels, under scaffolding platforms, and around guys in fluorescent green vests bearing down on jackhammers. On every corner billboards advertised one- and two-bedroom luxury condos. A defunct bank now housed a Heinen's grocery store. Rapid-transit buses stopped at futuristic stops along a downtown-to-East Side corridor. This was no longer the decrepit downtown that so easily matched my mood as my fortunes cratered with the Browns twenty or so years earlier. It was a city jumping off the life-support gurney and doing jumping jacks. But was it any more welcoming to failed ballplayers? I tried to remember the name of the woman I barhopped with that long-ago night. Failing, I permitted myself a final wallow in regret and entered Schiff's building through a revolving glass door.

I keep a navy-blue sports coat in my van alongside the Louisville Slugger for unscheduled visits such as this, but I still stood out like a Harold Robbins novel tucked between volumes of the Ohio Revised Code as I presented myself at a desk the size of a small yacht in the firm's lobby on the twentieth floor.

"Was Mr. Schiff expecting you?" the secretary helming the bridge asked me doubtfully. She wore a dark blouse and slacks, with lacquered red nails that could have deflected bullets and a pair of earrings that would have kept Hopalong in kibble for six months. She examined my card as if it were a laboratory slide containing a bubonic plague sample.

"I don't believe so. I just happened to be in town. It's a personal matter," I added, dropping my voice a notch.

"Personal?"

"It involves a mutual friend."

"And that would be?"

"A law school classmate of his. Her name is Laura Porter."

"I see. And you need—?"

"Just a couple minutes of his time. I know it's unorthodox, but my schedule is like a roller coaster these days. Up one day, down the next. You know how it is."

The look on her face indicated in fact she did not.

"If it's possible to just let him know I'm here?"

"Have a seat, please." She picked up the phone.

I didn't sit. I hiked across the waiting area and examined a framed late nineteenth-century map of greater Cleveland, yellowing and cracked but still in pretty good shape. I located Bay Front on the far west—nothing but a village in those days—and Shaker Heights on the east, where Schiff grew up. It wasn't often you heard of Clevelanders who passed from the east side across the great divide of downtown to settle on the west side, but I guess it could happen. Thanks to $2.65 million lakefront views, for example, which have a funny way of transcending neighborhood loyalties.

"Mr. Hayes?"

"Yes."

"Mr. Schiff has just a few minutes," the secretary said, disappointment in her eyes. "If you'll follow me."

She led me out of the lobby and down the hall past a series of wide cabinets whose open doors revealed pull-out drawers of hundreds of hanging files. On the opposite wall hung framed photographs—nearly all men—labeled as current and former firm partners. I spied authentic muttonchops on a turn-of-the-last century Raabe, and a fat 1970s tie on a young Northcott in a more recent portrait. At the end of the hallway the executive secretary stopped and directed me into a large office. I stepped inside. Randall P. Schiff stood up from his own oceangoing desk, walked around it and approached.

"Woody Hayes," he said, thrusting his right hand out to shake mine. "I don't believe it. We meet at last."

43

"HAVE A SEAT, PLEASE," Schiff said. "Can I get you anything?"

"I'm fine, thanks. I go by Andy now."

"Yes, yes, I should have realized. The Browns and all that were a long time ago, weren't they?"

"Yes, they were."

As he spoke I glanced at a framed poster on the wall, a blown-up photo of a capacity crowd at Ohio Stadium, a quintessential feature of thousands of offices around the state.

"Busted," Schiff said, following my gaze. "It's a bit of an obsession for us, isn't it?"

"There are worse," I said, wondering who he meant by "us."

"Just for the record, I never thought you got a fair shake up here. You didn't get enough credit for mounting a comeback. Everybody expected too much, too soon. That's always the way with Browns' fans, isn't it?"

"I suppose. But it's hard not to see their point."

"That's generous of you."

He swung the door of the office shut. I sat on a gray leather couch. He pulled a matching chair across the carpet and sat opposite me, a glass coffee table filled with glossy magazines between us. *Ohio Lawyer. The Economist. Forbes.* That day's *Wall Street Journal* and *New York Times*. Schiff picked up the *Times*, which lay the slightest bit askew, and set it down aligned with the *Journal*. He glanced at the closed door and then back to me.

"So what can I do for you? Eileen said something about Judge Porter? Is everything all right?"

"That's what I was hoping you could tell me."

"Anything I can do to help."

His face open, expression friendly. No hint of distrust. I found myself liking the guy, in spite of myself. In person, he was even better looking than the photo on the firm's website would lead you to believe. Tailored gray pinstripe suit, red power tie, black shoes glowing from a recent shine as if they were carved from polished ebony. His prematurely white hair, which might have suggested frailty in another man, gave him instead an aristocratic air that exuded power and virility. I contrasted him with Paul Thayer, whose picture I Googled within three nanoseconds of being with Laura for the first time. Schiff was the more conventionally handsome man: blue eyes, angular face, workout physique. But Thayer was far and away more interesting looking. Black hair tinged with gray and worn just the slightest bit long for a corporate lawyer; bushy eyebrows; perpetually exhausted eyes set deep within their sockets; hawk-like nose and striking chin. Even putting personality differences aside, it was easy to imagine a young Laura falling first for Schiff, with his all-American good looks, but then unsuccessfully fighting an attraction to the Heathcliff in the room.

Heathcliff. Dark hair, eyes set back in sockets, striking chin. A face I'd seen recently. A face—

"Andy? How may I help?"

I snapped back to attention, reluctantly setting aside the thought. I said, "Laura contacted me recently. Asked if I could help her out. We're old friends," I added.

"I didn't realize that. So this wasn't in your official capacity?"

"What do you mean?"

"You're an investigator now, aren't you? Private?"

Pawn to queen's bishop 4. A solid opening. A lot of Ohioans who hear my name know what I did as a football player—or didn't do, depending on their perspective. Far fewer know my current occupation. The fact that Schiff did could mean almost anything, but it was an interesting gambit. Now I had to figure out how to counter.

"That's right. And as a matter of fact, I am working for Laura."

"Let me guess. Something to do with her campaign?"

The question of the week, apparently.

"Something along those lines. She led me to believe she's in some kind of trouble."

"Trouble?"

"That's what she said. I'm just wondering if you know what she meant by that?"

"Me? Why would I know?"

"Well, you're supporting her candidacy, for one thing. According to campaign finance filings, anyway. That made me wonder if you've been in touch."

"You've done your homework. And since you have, I assure you my support's on the up and up."

"But have you—"

A nearly imperceptible glance at the closed door. "She didn't say what this trouble was?"

"No."

"And you think because I'm supporting her, I know something?"

"Do you?"

"I know she's a good judge. That's about it, I'm afraid."

I thought about bringing up his business card in the van by the barn. Instead I tried a different tack. "Let me ask you this. The donations you made."

"What about them?"

"One appeared to be in a private capacity, during the primary. The second, more recent one, came back to an address connected to a company called PG Inc."

That won me a small blink. "That's right."

"If I may ask, do you work for them?"

"If you don't mind me saying, these are unusual questions for an unannounced visit in the middle of the day."

"That's fair, and I hate to bother you with all this. It just happened that I was up here and realized I had an opening."

"I'm sure your schedule's more elastic than mine," he said with a smile. "I envy you, in a way. As far as PG is concerned, it's more a situation of *doing* work for them. I'm on retainer as counsel. Why are you bringing this up, if I may ask?"

"The thing is—as I'm sure you know—PG Inc. and Rumford share an address. And since Rumford is involved in the Mendon Woods lawsuit—"

"I see. You're wondering if I'm involved in that too."

"Well, you or that company. Strictly from a campaign finance perspective," I added quickly. "I don't care about the lawsuit or the swamp—I have a thing about mosquitoes. It's just a question of the perception of impropriety."

"What do you mean?" His voice harder now.

"Your campaign donation. And others that connect back to PG Inc., and hence to the developer. Whether, to be frank, there's an attempt to unduly influence the judge. There could be a lot at stake."

"At stake how?"

I mentioned Flota, the European AI company. The scuttled project in Indiana—maybe looking for a home elsewhere?

He leaned back. "The implication is that Rumford wants Judge Porter to rule in their favor in the lawsuit and is bundling donations to provide her incentive."

"If you put it that way, yes."

"I don't think it's a state secret Rumford wants that land. It's why they went to court."

"But what about PG Inc.? What's their interest—or is it yours? And is it connected to—"

"This is where client confidentiality enters the picture, I'm afraid."

"But am I correct that PG or Flota or both also have an interest in Mendon Woods? PG is a cloud-computing company, right? It builds warehouses of a sort, but for information, not tangible things? Like AI?"

Schiff looked at me for several seconds before replying.

"What an interesting question," he said.

44

OUTSIDE AND FAR BELOW, I heard jackhammers and a single police siren. Through Schiff's closed office door I caught the sound of laughter, a couple of manly voices sharing a joke. A moment later I felt my phone buzzing in my pocket.

"Information warehouses. Well, that's simplifying things a bit," Schiff said. "I like to think of them as information *banks,* because information is the new currency, isn't it? He glanced at the magazines on the coffee table. "It's also the future, pure and simple. You've heard of Bitcoin?"

"The virtual currency?"

He nodded. "Right now companies are competing to build warehouses in Iceland to digitally mine the currency. A massive new economic segment based on something tremendously lucrative but completely intangible."

I thought of Gloria and her Alexa bot, the one her grandkids liked to talk to—and accidentally order toy horses from. Of talking toasters. Of another article I'd read while researching this mess—that artificial intelligence was helping Facebook translate *billions* of conversations from one language to another each day. The size of the place needed to store the chips to power all that intelligence. *Someplace big,* according to Bonnie. Then I thought of something else she said.

"Isn't that why they call the company Flota?" I said. "Named for the fleet that brought New World gold to Europe? That age's new riches?"

"Very good, Andy. They couldn't build ships fast enough in those days. Just like the server farms of today, I suppose."

"Well put."

"Thank you. Stop me if I get carried away. My partners say I have tunnel vision on the topic."

"It's understandable. But like I said, I don't really care if you or PG Inc. has an interest in that swamp—"

"As I said, it's not something I'm able to—"

"I only care if Laura might be endangered by your enthusiasm."

The choice of verb was a gamble, but the payoff was there, if slight. The twitch in Schiff's left eye was more subtle than the corresponding twitch to Gloria's mouth, and not nearly so cute. I almost missed it. Knight to KB2. Check.

"Endangered?"

"Her campaign, I mean. Back to the question of an appearance of impropriety."

My phone buzzed again. I retrieved it, saw it was Theresa calling, and sent the call to voice mail.

"I can assure you I wouldn't do anything that puts Laura's campaign at risk. She's an old friend of mine, too. My donation was in the interest of supporting someone I know and respect."

"And the donations of the other five PG Inc. principals?"

"What about them?"

"Are they interested in supporting an old friend? Or making a calculated statement about a decision they'd like her to make?"

"Respect is a powerful motivator, Andy. In sports, as I'm sure you know, but in business, especially. I can't speak for my colleagues' decisions, monetary or otherwise. But like-minded isn't the same as misguided, if that makes sense."

"So it's a coincidence so many people from a company connected to the developer in Laura's lawsuit made sizable campaign donations to her."

"It's neither coincidence nor intentionality. It's a fact, and one whose conclusions you'd have to explore with each individual." He glanced at his watch. "And now, I'm sorry, but I have an appointment. It's a busy day. With all due respect, you're lucky I had this time slot free."

"Have you been to the Mansfield area recently?"

He stared at me. "I'm sorry?"

I repeated the question.

"I've passed it on the way to Columbus. Now if you don't mind—"

"Do you know someone named Gary Phipps? From Springfield, Missouri?"

"I don't believe so. Friend of yours?"

"More of a frenemy, I think. How about—"

"I appreciate you coming by," he said, standing abruptly. "I'm afraid our time is up." He walked around the chair, opened his office door, and waited for me to rise. I followed suit reluctantly.

"Are you sure—"

"Let me say this," Schiff said. "I regret losing touch with Laura personally. I've followed her career from a distance with great admiration. Harming her prospects is the last thing I want to do."

I said, "Laura was the Berman Prize winner at Ohio State. Isn't that right?"

"I'm sorry?"

"The scholarship. Laura was your class's Berman Prize recipient."

"I'm not sure what that has to do with anything. And as I said, I have—"

"You also applied, if I'm not mistaken."

"How would you know that?"

"And just to clarify—you and Laura are more than old friends, correct? You dated at one time. Before she and Paul Thayer became a couple."

Storm clouds entered and departed his eyes like a fast-forwarded film of a Lake Erie squall. If I hadn't been looking carefully I would have missed them.

"These are personal matters, and also ancient history, Andy. I'm not sure why you're bringing this up. I was happy to answer your questions about the campaign and PG Inc. But two-decades-old affairs of the heart? Really? Is that the kind of digging you do?"

"It can't have been easy losing Laura to Paul, knowing you'd also lost the Berman Prize to her. Which makes it seem odd."

"Makes what seem odd?" Voice as cold as the air temperature during that lake squall.

"That you'd stay friends with her, afterward. Help her out with papers and exams?"

"I really don't think—"

"Laura was under a lot of stress in those days. Struggled with deadlines. Something you saw you could help her with? But why?"

He was wrestling with a response when a knock at the door interrupted us. Eileen, a pair of thick manila folders in her hands.

"I'm sorry, Mr. Schiff. You told me—"

He reached out and took the folders. "Thank you. Mr. Hayes was just leaving."

"Was I?"

"I believe so. Eileen will show you out."

I glanced at the executive secretary. Weighed my options. I was pretty sure I could outmuscle her, although it's possible she took weekend jiujitsu classes and I'd end up flat on my back. Plus I've always had a thing for lacquered nails, and there was a chance she'd bedazzle me without warning. Then where would I be? As far as Schiff was concerned, the look on his face when I brought up the Berman Prize and Paul told me everything I needed to know—short of whether his taxidermist was doing a rush job on a coastal tanager for his mantel.

"Thanks for seeing me," I said, headed for the door.

"Andy?"

I turned.

"I said before I wasn't sure you received a fair shake when you were up here."

"Yes?"

"You may have gotten what you deserved after all."

45

SAFELY PAST MUTTON CHOPS and 1970s Tie and
ensconced in an express elevator ride downstairs, I pulled out my
phone and hit redial for Theresa.

"So what do you think, QB?" she said when she picked up.

"About what?"

"About the kid. Daniel. The judge's son."

"What about him?"

"Didn't you get my message?"

"I saw you called, but I was in a meeting. I didn't—"

"What's the point of having voice mail if you don't listen to
your messages?"

"What's the situation? I'm listening now."

"The situation, QB, is he's missing."

"Who?"

"Daniel. He's gone."

WE REACHED THE FIRST floor. I told Theresa to wait
a moment as I exited. I pocketed the phone, pushed through a
revolving door, stood for a moment on Euclid, took my bearings,
and walked across the street. I entered a PNC Bank branch with
a view of the entrance of Schiff's building. I pulled a deposit slip
out of a plastic tray and placed it on the glass desk and lifted a

PNC pen from a tray of handouts. I tried to remember the last time I filled out a paper deposit slip. Obama's first term came to mind. To leave the impression of an actual bank customer as opposed to someone conducting surveillance, I started writing on the slip. I wrote the opening lines of "My Town," the ode to Cleveland by native son Michael Stanley. I got as far as *This old town . . .* and retrieved the phone.

"Sorry about that."

"What's going on? Did you hear what I said?"

"Loud and clear. Talk to me."

"That's what I'm trying to do. The kid's not at his apartment. His roommate said he didn't come home last night. He thought it was a little weird and called the gym, and they didn't know either."

"The gym?"

"World Fitness, in some plaza up in Clintonville. Where he works. But he didn't show up today."

"Does he have a car?"

"A beater, an old Toyota. The roommate showed me where it's usually parked. It's not around."

I returned to the thought I had in Schiff's office, comparing what I remembered of Daniel from the picture of him and his sister by Laura's bedside to Paul Thayer. Bushy eyebrows; perpetually exhausted eyes set deep within their sockets; hawk-like nose and prominent chin. I summoned the partial photo I spied on Laura's phone as it rang in her car. *My God—are you all right?* The same day SouthSideMama99 said her daughter's boyfriend took an emergency call for new locks at Daniel's apartment. Now it came to me: the man in the caller ID photo had the same deep-set eyes and hawk-like nose.

Of course. The judge's son was the person who called that night. The person the judge had to go see, just for an hour or so. Except the hour turned into two turned into . . . what?

Accidents happen.

Calm down. It's at least an hour from Columbus.

I said, "Can you check the gym?"

"Duh, QB. That's where I'm going next. I just wanted to touch base first."

"Thanks—I really appreciate it."

"You think something happened to him?"

"I'm not sure. He could be in trouble. He could also be sleeping off a bender in somebody else's apartment—he's young and a bit aimless. Let's see what the people at the gym say."

"All right. Just check your voice mail next time, all right?"

"I'll try—"

I stopped. Across the street, Randall P. Schiff emerged from a revolving door and started down the street, on foot and in a hurry. No sign of a briefcase, let alone the folders Eileen handed to him that seemed so important just a few minutes ago.

"Gotta go. Let me know about the gym."

"That actually occurred to me to do, QB—"

I disconnected. I crumpled up the deposit slip and tossed it in the trash. I couldn't remember the rest of the lyrics anyway. But I recalled something else. "My Town" was blasting from the concourse as I suited up on the last day I ever played for the Browns.

I FOLLOWED SCHIFF TWO blocks before I ended the pursuit as he entered a parking garage off Prospect and disappeared inside. This was pointless. Even if I sprinted to my own garage, the chances of paying, exiting, and driving back here in time to follow him were minimal. If my suspicions were correct, there were only two places he could be headed to. And the first—a swamp in Mohican County—seemed too long a drive on the spur of the moment.

I walked toward Chestnut and my van. On the way I called Gloria. After she picked up, I told her about my conversation with Schiff, and then what Theresa found when she went to Daniel's apartment. I relayed my certainty he was the one who called the judge that night.

She said, "You think they snatched him?"

"I don't know. He could have gone to ground on his own, maybe switched apartments at his mom's advice."

194

"But why do that if they changed the locks?"

"A good point, unfortunately. Then there's those guys in the barn last night, talking about someone coming from Columbus. Maybe somebody was on the way up with her son."

"But why take him?"

"Leverage, maybe? Show Laura they're serious?"

"More serious than a dead bird on a kitchen table?"

"There's a reason she's called the Velvet Fist. I'm thinking she drove up here to confront Schiff the other night, after dealing with Daniel. Maybe she thought she could negotiate her way out of the situation and they made it clear to her she can't."

"That's a scary thought, if they took her son," Gloria said. "Especially—"

"Especially because of Todd Orick. I know."

"So are you thinking what I'm thinking? He's in the barn?"

"Isolated and secure. As we both know."

"I'll swing by as soon as I can, check if I can see anything. I'm jammed up at the moment."

"What's wrong?"

"The chief's got me running radar on Route 13. Speaking of making things clear."

"I don't follow."

"Young guys usually get that gig. It's almost like he wants me out of pocket."

"You think he knows—"

"Knows that you and I were sneaking through cornfields last night? No idea. Doubtful, you ask me. But he may be under extra pressure. Knowing you were here may have everybody nervous."

"Let's hope that's all it is. All right—just let me know."

"What are you going to do?"

"I'm going to take a walk."

"A walk?"

"A stroll on the beach, actually."

46

I THOUGHT ABOUT DETOURING past Browns Stadium before heading to my next destination, but decided that was a poor use of time. Far better to repeatedly bash my head with a two-pound engineer hammer. Instead, I drove back onto the highway and followed signs for I-90 West. I exited at Detroit Avenue and cut down Wagar to Lake Avenue. I turned left, and a few minutes later entered the city limits of Bay Front, Ohio.

Once upon a time, the town served as a summer destination for well-off, water-loving Clevelanders seeking relief from the city's heat and grime, especially in the days when steel mills choked the skies with the soot of economic progress. As a result, many of the homes lining the streets and overlooking the lake were modest forties- and fifties-era bungalows—winterized beach houses, in essence. But that was only half the story. Money had come to Bay Front as a bedroom community in the era of the Great Commute. Numerous lakeshore houses were not-so-modest mansions built on plots—sometimes two or three packaged together—that once held those small bungalows before they were demolished to make room for something far bigger and more luxurious. That was the gilded Bay Front, one of the more exclusive greater Cleveland exurbs.

Schiff's place fell into the latter category of homes, I saw, coming up on the house on my right. I stopped, threw on my flashers, and examined the residence. Up front, close to the street, a wrought-iron driveway gate stretched across the drive, a large S embedded in the middle. A gate it would take some doing to get past. Behind that, a downward-sloping asphalt drive. Farther down, partly obscured by dogwoods and evergreens, a house whose three levels of wood, stone, and glass seemed to float over the edge of a lakeside cliff like a freeze-frame photo of a house collapsing mid-earthquake. I estimated the distance from the street to the house at a hundred yards, give or take. On a hunch, I dug into my pocket and retrieved Laura's extra car fob, taken two mornings before from her condo. I glanced in my rearview mirror and saw a police car approaching. Quickly, I stretched out my hand and activated the fob.

Meep meep.

The sound was far away and indistinct, like a cat's mewing from two houses over. But also unquestionable. Laura's Lexus was on Schiff's property behind one of the three garage doors below.

I turned off the flashers and drove away slowly, hoping to leave the impression of someone who'd stopped to check directions. I was guessing Bay Front was not a city where police took kindly to palookas in vans with big butts casing houses. The cop followed me two blocks before turning left into a private drive of condominiums. I exhaled and drove another few blocks before turning right into a small city park.

I waited until I was sure the officer hadn't just circled around. Satisfied, I texted Gloria the news of discovering Laura's car. Without checking for a reply, I locked up and walked to the railing overlooking the lake. A slight midafternoon breeze kicked up small ripples of water all the way to the horizon. In the distance a silhouette of a barge working its way to Canada. Closer up a trio of sailboats leaning to the side, like white table napkins thrown into the wind. On the shore a small bird with spindly legs—sandpiper?—ran here and there as if attached to an off-stage string. It would have been pleasant to stand like that all afternoon, contemplating the universe instead of battling its dark forces. Putting the thought aside, I glanced around to assure myself I was alone, then followed the railing to a set of descending concrete stairs. Two minutes later I was on a patch of ground covered with gritty sand, stones, and driftwood; what passed for a beach in this part of the world. I turned to my right and started walking.

The going was tough. The shore of Lake Erie, like Cleveland itself, doesn't suffer fools gladly. At points I was nearly in the water, balancing on rocks and grabbing branches of small bushes sprouting from the cliffside to keep from soaking myself. Along other stretches the shore widened enough that I came across metal fire rings and picnic tables. Once or twice I spied rickety wooden staircases winding their way to the houses perched atop the cliff. None of the stairways looked capable of supporting the weight of anything heavier than Hopalong. After another few minutes I came to a smaller promontory and stopped. I retrieved my phone and pulled up the GPS. I was just about there. I stepped around the promontory and looked up. And found myself staring at Randall P. Schiff.

I DUCKED BACK, THOUGH I was pretty sure he hadn't seen me. His eyes were on the horizon, not the beach, as mine had been minutes earlier in the park. He'd driven quickly from downtown and couldn't have been home long. Score one for my intuition. But had he heard the *meep meep* of Laura's car? His presence outside would suggest not, but could I know for sure? I eased myself back into position to see without being seen. He was still there, looking out at the lake at the edge of an impressive-looking deck cantilevered over the cliff like the prow of a nineteenth-century sailing ship. The only thing it lacked was a carved maiden casting her eternal gaze over the water. Schiff's own rickety-looking set of stairs led to the beach, where a ridge of sharp-edged boulders jutted from the shoreline, severely cutting down on sandcastle possibilities.

I thought: Was the judge in the house? Was this where she'd driven after the call from her son? And was she here when she lied to Pinney at the sheriff's office, and then dropped the clues that led me on this path?

I snuck a final glance at the deck and ducked back immediately. Schiff was no longer alone. He'd been joined by Tear Drop. Which complicated the idea forming in my mind a moment earlier, to just barge in and rescue Laura—if she wanted rescuing at all. I waited a minute and peeked once more. Now the deck was empty. A moment later I heard a sound. It took me a second—a garage door opening. A moment after that the scrape of metal that indicated the driveway fence sliding open. Someone was leaving—but who?

I hurried back toward the park and my van, keeping close to the cliff overlooking the lake in case anyone from above was spying on midday beachcombers. I was nearly back to the park when my phone rang. Pete Henderson was on the line, calling from the U.S. Attorney's Office.

47

"IS THAT A SEAGULL?" Henderson said. "Where are you?"

"I believe that's a ring-billed gull." The bird hung motionless in the air overhead as it rode an air current. "It's the de facto Ohio gull—sort of like the white-tailed deer of the skies." Ring-billed gull: yet another factoid gleaned from my not-a-birder father. "To answer your question, I'm in Cleveland."

"Cleveland? That's out of our jurisdiction. Like that's going to help my boss."

"I'll do right by your boss, trust me. Did you find anything out?"

"Oh yeah. I found out there's a reason why you wanted someone doing your dirty work."

"Dirty work? I told you—"

"Skip it. So this Berman Prize thing? That's a sweeter deal than I realized. Wish I'd applied."

"Could you have won?"

"Not a chance. And even if I had, I could never have kept it. The GPA requirement's a bitch. I nearly failed con law."

"That's comforting. So what about Laura? Anything?"

"Let's start with that DOJ internship the judge got. Those don't grow on trees. You need juice to pull those down."

"What kind of juice?"

"*Juice* juice. Like you need to be seriously connected. It takes a gold-plated recommendation—federal judge or forget it."

"And Laura had that?"

"Yup."

"Who was the judge?"

"Northcott."

"Who?"

"Federal bench down here. You might not know him. He's emeritus now, only does a couple cases a year."

"Hang on. Did you say Northcott?"

"That's right. The Honorable George."

I recalled the fragment of a business card found in a van. A 1970s tie as wide as the Champs-Élysées. Schiff's firm: Raabe, Karabinus, Northcott, Rickard and Dowd.

"Could Northcott have a relative who's a lawyer? Maybe a brother?"

"Possibly. Why?"

Carefully, I said, "I ran into someone named Randall Schiff who works in a law firm where a Northcott's a partner."

"How's that guy connected to any of this?"

"It's a little complicated. And it could be nothing. So you said this judge wrote Laura a recommendation?"

"That's what I'm told."

"By who?"

"By someone at the law school who owes *me* a favor. You're not the only wheeler and dealer in town, you know."

"The title's all yours. Back to that judge. Do you know why he wrote the recommendation? Did he know Laura?"

"No idea. You'd have to ask him yourself."

"I guess I will, thanks."

"Good luck with that."

"Why?"

"Let's just say he hasn't got a reputation as a people person. He was a real stickler for decorum. And by stickler I mean asshole—suits for male lawyers, skirts for female lawyers, otherwise take a hike. Frankly, I was a little surprised he wrote anything to help Laura out—or anyone, for that matter. Now, mind telling me what all this is about?"

Overhead the ring-billed gull dipped its wings and floated to the shoreline, where it searched for food with quick, probing jabs of its bill. I regretted not bringing along a bag of Cheetos, its traditional diet.

"I can't. Not just yet."

"You've got to be kidding me. After the limb I went out on? The favor I called in? My law school contact had to do some digging."

"I'm sorry, Pete. It's a sensitive situation right now."

"Sure it is. Sounds like your version of 'It's not me, it's you.'"

"I promise I'll fill you in as soon as—"

"Listen carefully. If this comes back to bite me, and I have squat from you as collateral, you've placed your last call to this office."

"I just need a little more time."

"For what? To think of more ways to screw me over?"

I heard a beep and saw Theresa was calling.

"I've got to take another call. I'll be back in touch, Pete. Promise—"

"Promise, my ass," he said, and disconnected.

48

I MOUNTED THE STEPS to the parking lot and hurried to my van as I listened to Theresa's report on the gym where the judge's son worked.

"I ran into trouble as soon as I got there, QB."

"Trouble?"

"This little busybody was running the desk. One of these size two girls with attitude, like the fact they work out and don't eat meat and wear fluorescent underwear in public means they've accomplished something in life. She wouldn't give me the time of day. I asked about Daniel, if she could tell me when he last worked, if anybody knew where he was or had heard from him. All that. She just put on that resting-bitch face they all have and shut me down."

I sighed in frustration. Theresa had come far from her days on the streets. But there were times when her roots reemerged with a vengeance. Plus, her thrift-store outfits didn't always help her cause—a style I referred to privately as Pippi Longstocking chic. I wondered whether the girl at the desk was reacting to any of that, though I didn't bring it up.

"I'm sorry about—"

"Hang onto your drawers, QB," Theresa continued. "So I'm like, let me talk to the manager. Should have seen her face then.

But I'm not letting up, and eventually she wiggles off into the gym and she comes back with this big guy. He takes one look at me and I can tell it's my lucky day. I hike up my chest and repeat the questions, making sure I'm sticking my boobs at him like all get out—"

"Theresa—"

"And the whole time that girl's doing a slow burn behind him. Because I'm guessing she wishes he looked at her that way, only he doesn't, because she doesn't have boobs like mine. He tells me yeah, Daniel missed his shift, no call, nothing, and do I know anything. I explain I'm looking for him too, and ask about Daniel's car, if he's seen it, and he's like, 'Sure, let's check it out.' So we go into the parking lot and look around. And the whole time he's asking me if I ever go to a gym, or would I ever consider a personal trainer, and he'd be happy to work something out with me, maybe something on the side if my schedule's tight. I'm thinking, yeah, you'd be happy. In your dreams. But I don't say nothing, just keep nodding and smiling and sticking my—"

"I get the picture—"

"And guess what?"

"What?"

"That kid's car is parked in the lot. On the end of the row. As far as we could tell, where he left it when he came to work yesterday."

"You mean?"

"I don't think that judge's son ever got out of the parking lot, QB."

I opened up the van, unlocked it and slid into the driver's seat.

"QB?"

"Yeah."

"You there?"

"Yeah. That's good work, Theresa. Unorthodox technique, but good."

"Unorthodox? A girl pushing out her chest to get a guy to talk? That's like private eye 101. Maybe I should be giving you some tips."

"Maybe you should. Listen, can you hang tight for a couple hours? In case I need anything else?"

"I gotta get back to the church. I'm supervising a GED class at three. I'll keep my eye on my phone. What are you going to do?"

I turned and glanced through the van window at the shoreline, where more gulls were now circling.

"Run some interference, I think."

"What's that mean?"

"When I figure it out I'll let you know."

I SAT AND PONDERED the coincidence that Henderson's digging produced. A judge named Northcott wrote Laura her recommendation for the DOJ internship—winning which helped her keep her scholarship. Two decades on, she was in some kind of trouble involving former classmate and boyfriend Randall P. Schiff, who worked for a law firm whose partners included a Northcott. I did a quick Google search on my phone and confirmed that attorney Samuel Northcott and federal judge George Northcott were indeed brothers. Both in their late seventies by now. Strange. And wasn't a Northcott one of Schiff's neighbors in Shaker Heights? Stranger still. I thought about calling Henderson back to ask one more favor. But the end of our conversation made me think that would be what we trained investigators call a brick wall. Instead, I looked up Judge Northcott's number and dialed it myself. I was trying to conjure up another alias when an automatic prompt requested that I leave a message. After a moment of hesitation I did so, providing my name and number and a vague explanation about a law school scholarship question. Even as I did so, I thought of the *meep meep* of Laura's car in Schiff's garage, and whether all this work was in vain. What if I had it all wrong? What if Laura was fine and once again I was rushing in like a fool where I didn't belong?

Or what if she was in trouble, she and her son, seriously deep shit trouble, and it was already too late to help?

49

I FIGURED I'D WAIT a few minutes and then call Schiff's office to see if he'd returned. If he had, that would buy me time while I thought about how to get myself inside his house to satisfy myself one way or the other. Before I had a chance to consider that or any other options, movement on my left caught my attention. A Bay Front Police Department cruiser pulled into the parking lot and stopped on the far side. The cop in the passenger seat looked out at the lake and then casually glanced in my direction. Too casually, I realized. Sometimes you can just tell when you're made. I started the van, backed up slowly, and just as casually drove toward the park exit, trying to keep my heart on an even keel. One cop? Coincidence. Two? Speaking of juice, I was guessing Schiff had some around here, if only to judge by his day job and the size of his lakeshore crib. Someone had the cops' attention. They might not have known to look for a used Honda Odyssey with a big butt. But I was guessing they had a decent description of me.

Satisfied I wasn't being followed, I retreated up the road to the Bay Diner, a restaurant that had among many things going for it the fact it served breakfast all day. I squeezed into a booth, grabbed a menu, and pulled out my phone. A waitress brought me water, utensils, and coffee, hesitated for a moment, hovering, then departed when I said I needed more time. I made my decision and put the menu down. She was back in a flash.

"What can I get you, hon?"

I ordered a cheese omelet, home fries, and bacon. She wrote down the order, took the menu from me, and said, "Aren't you Woody Hayes? Played for the Browns?"

I nodded slowly. "These days I go by Andy—"

"You really sucked when you were up here. Bit the big one, you know?"

"I'm sorry—"

"It's good to see you back. My sister and I had the biggest crush on you. You were the cutest of any of them. Any chance you could—"

She held out her order pad and a pen. I looked and saw she was blushing.

"I'd be happy to. What's your sister's name?"

She said it was Ellen. She was Claire. I signed individual autographs to both of them.

"I really appreciate it," she said, grinning at the signature. "Ellen's gonna die when I tell her. And I'll have that omelet right up, hon. *Woody,*" she added with a giggle.

I shook my head as she left, dwelling once more on what might have been. Fortunately for my ill-advised remembrance of things past, I was interrupted by Gloria calling in.

"Something's up," she said.

I TOOK A SIP of water, sat back, and listened while she talked.

"I snuck away from radar duty long enough to swing past the barn. I saw the van back there, parked outside. Same one as last night. And another car pulled in after that."

"You see anyone?"

"I was too far off."

When she was finished I explained what Theresa learned by visiting Daniel Thayer's apartment and then the gym.

"Is *she* your girlfriend?"

"Who?"

"That girl. Theresa."

"I told you, I don't have a girlfriend. I thought I made that clear last night."

"You made plenty clear last night, Hayes. And this morning. Who is she, then?"

"She's an ex-prostitute who works part-time for me when she's not rescuing trafficked women."

"I would have settled for girlfriend. You've got some unusual coworkers, I'll give you that. I didn't even know roller derby still existed until you told me about your computer lady. So what are we going to do?"

"I'm not sure. I'm afraid the chances they have the judge's son in that barn are good at this point."

"Agreed. But why?"

"Leverage, like I said. Make clear how important it is for her to rule against the swamp."

"They'll never get away with this, Hayes. It's too outlandish."

"You and I know that. But maybe they think they've got Laura in a corner. And maybe she didn't help her case by deciding not to go to the police in the first place. Maybe that's why they think this will work."

"If any of this is true, we've got to go in there. Get that boy. I'm not—"

"Not what?"

"I got a call from Todd Orick's folks today. They asked me if anything else was happening. Anything that came out of your visit. I'm not going through that again."

I lowered my phone and looked at the time. I said, "Thing is, I'm an hour away, minimum. And I'm not sure it's a good idea to leave here, with the judge in the house."

"I could probably get some backup. But I'm not sure it would be enough."

"Backup? Who?"

"My ex. I told you he's on the job with Mansfield City. What I didn't tell you was he went to high school with Todd Orick's uncle. He took this hard as anybody."

"Would he help you? With something like this?"

"We're not archenemies, Hayes. We just couldn't live together. He'd be up for it, sure. But even him and me, I don't know—"

"Hang on. What if I could get you some reinforcements?"

"Like who?"

"Like somebody. Another coworker."

"Not another girlfriend."

"He's not a girlfriend. And he's got a buddy. And there's a big difference between this guy and me."

"What would that be?"

"For starters, he carries a gun."

I HUNG UP AND called Otto. I cursed, getting his voice mail, but started to leave a message anyway. Before I finished he called me back.

"Woody. What's up, brother?"

"Are you still in Ashland?"

"For about five more minutes. Me and Big Dog stopped in at Grandpa's Cheese Barn. I'm running low on beef jerky."

I rolled my eyes. The specialty country store was just off the highway, at the same exit with the sign that proclaimed Ashland the world capital of nice people.

"Pick me up some Amish peanut butter while you're at it. The kind they mix the marshmallow fluff into. You finished with your job?"

"Easy peasy, once we got to him. Grandma was the tough one. Anyway, he's on ice in the city jail."

"Yeah, gotta be careful of grandmas. So why aren't you transporting him?"

"He's got two warrants up here. Ashland County and Franklin County get to arm wrestle for who arraigns him first. Long as I get paid, I don't care who's providing his pillow. What's going on?"

I explained why I was calling. Most people would have a question or two about a plan that involved invading a barn in the middle of nowhere occupied by an unknown number of enemy combatants. Otto listened without interruption.

When I finished, he said, "Me, Big Dog, the lady cop, and her ex-husband, who's also a cop? Odds aren't good, Woody."

"I know it's a big ask—"

"I mean, odds aren't good for whoever's in that barn holding the kid. But just for the heck of it, any other locals we can pull in? Make it all official?"

I told him Gloria's fears that Mohican County authorities and perhaps even her own department were compromised.

"She knows you're calling me?"

"Yes."

"Is this a charity gig?"

"Maybe. I'm in fundraising mode at the moment."

"In other words, yes. OK, text me her number."

"Thanks, Otto. Keep in touch, all right? And let me know as soon as—"

"As soon as we rescue the kid. No shit, Woody. Over and out, and all that jazz."

What I'd been going to say was, As soon as you find him, one way or the other.

50

I SENT OTTO GLORIA'S number. The message
went through just as Claire brought me my food. She thanked
me again for the autographs. I nodded and said anytime. When
she was gone I tucked into breakfast. I hadn't realized how hun-
gry I was. It had been a long time since toast and yogurt and . . .
and the morning at Gloria's. Assured I would survive at least until
a midnight snack, I was preparing to call Schiff's firm when my
phone rang again. A Columbus exchange.

"I'm calling from Judge Northcott's office," a woman said.
"You left a message."

"Yes. Thanks for calling me back."

Dead air.

After a second I said, "I just had a quick question about"—
about what exactly?—"about, as odd as this may sound, a recommendation the judge wrote for a friend of mine."

To my surprise, she said, "Is this about the Berman Prize?"

"Yes, as a matter of fact. But how—"

"I've already answered the question once this month. This
has to do with the judge?"

"Judge Northcott? Yes—"

"Not Judge Northcott. Judge *Porter*."

"Judge Porter?"

A deep sigh. "No offense, whoever you are, but I don't appreciate you taking up my time and Judge Northcott's time with this. I already informed the judge that she was mistaken. Anything more, you'll have to get from her."

"Mistaken? About what?"

"The recommendation letter she called about."

"Judge Porter called about—"

"We've checked all the files. Judge Northcott didn't write any such letter. And that's all I have to say on it. And now I have to go."

And with that she hung up.

I SAT BACK, MIND reeling.

Judge Northcott didn't write Laura a recommendation letter for the Berman Prize? Then how—?

I considered what the woman told me—that Laura herself had called, inquiring. But why? To ask a retired judge twenty years after the fact about a recommendation letter he wrote her? That made no sense. Except—if the letter wasn't real. But if it wasn't real, where did it come from? Could Laura have faked it, and checked to see what if anything the judge suspected? Perhaps covering her tracks with the campaign on? Such cheating seemed utterly out of character. Yet her ex-husband mentioned she'd struggled with deadlines in those days. A mistake made out of desperation? Forging the letter at the last second to score an internship that both saved her scholarship and secured her future? It might explain the frame wedged into the wastebasket in her home office. Had the enormity of her misdeed finally hit home? Or was there—

A new thought came to me. What if Schiff discovered Laura's wrongdoing? Maybe through the Northcott in his firm? What if that was the approach he made, needing something to force Laura's hand on Mendon Woods, desperate to cut a deal favorable to PG Inc. and, by extension, Flota? The revelation of such dishonesty on Laura's part, even two decades old, would be disastrous if made public. It would make her Supreme Court opponent's mini-scandal—the fudged continuing-ed hours—look like a filched paper clip by comparison. And a forged recommendation would do more than wreck Laura's campaign. It could destroy her judicial career and jeopardize her law license. She'd be forced at her age to start all over again.

But yet. She resisted. She didn't go along with Schiff. She called me instead. *I need your help . . . I'm in trouble.* And it was then that Schiff increased the pressure. His demands were no longer about her. He moved on to her family. On to her son. Because the stakes were high. Because when it came to Mendon Woods, we weren't talking more strip plazas. We were talking the possibility of a giant AI installation. Economic impact on steroids. What was it Bonnie e-mailed me?

That's the funny thing about AI. It takes a lot of humans to make it work.

A lot of humans. A lot of jobs. I thought of something else I'd read, that AI specialists could pull down half a million dollars in salary and stock. A project like this would be a hugely lucrative prize for Columbus—and for Schiff.

I thought again of the Berman Prize. How it must have seemed a stain on Laura's past she couldn't bear to stare at any longer, not to mention the professional disaster it foretold. No wonder she trashed it. But why reach out to me? To intervene somehow? Shut Schiff up? Maybe not literally, but to help her negotiate a way out of this mess? And maybe that's what would have happened, until her son called her as we steamed up the windows in her Lexus. *Accidents happen.* One thing was certain. The sooner I could get myself into Schiff's house, the better. I finished my last piece of bacon, drank some coffee, found the number for Schiff's firm on my phone, and dialed. A few seconds later I found myself speaking with my old friend Eileen.

"This is Charlie Bauman," I said, lowering my voice. "Calling for Mr. Schiff."

"I'm sorry, Mr.—"

"Bauman."

"Could you spell that?"

I did. And told her it was important.

"May I ask the nature of your call?"

I grasped at straws. "It's about his apartment complex. In Parma? There's a problem with the plumbing. It won't take long. Is he available?"

"He's with someone right at the moment."

"I can hold."

"All right," she said, doubtfully. A moment later classical music came onto the line.

I hung up. That was good enough for me. Schiff had retreated to his office, perhaps—probably?—after checking up on the judge. Which meant I had a little time, since Gloria's shift ended at eight and it would take her and Otto a couple minutes after that to get in place. I felt guilty, delegating such a big job to them. But there was only so much I could do at this point. My new concern was finding a place to wait for the next couple of hours until Otto and crew did their thing and I could enter Schiff's house under cover of darkness.

I was trying to decide how to proceed, and thinking again of the possibility that Laura's entire career was based on a fraud. Finally, unable to bear it, I called Pete Henderson back. Who cared about his bruised feelings? Not surprisingly, I got voice mail. I asked him for one more favor, explaining that lives could be at stake. I needed him to check one more thing about a former Ohio State law student and a federal judge. Feeling as hopeless as I had at any point in this investigation—up to and including my self-flagellation over my lost chances with the Browns—I disconnected.

I was looking for Claire to signal for the check when I happened to glance through the restaurant window at the street. A Bay Front police cruiser was driving slowly past the diner. Third time the charm? I held my breath, looked toward the back of the restaurant for an exit, and relaxed as the cruiser passed. Claire approached a moment later.

"Anything else, hon?"

"Just the check. And, listen—any idea where there's a computer I could get access to around here?"

"A computer?"

"To check the internet. And hang out for a while."

"Library's up the street."

"Maybe someplace less public."

She gave me a funny look. "Afraid somebody might not want you back up here?"

"Something like that."

She thought for a second. "My nephew works at the Apple Store, over at Crocker Park mall. That's right around the corner. I bet he'd let you get on a computer. They got a million of them."

I thought about it. A mall on a weekday afternoon in the summer. Hiding in plain sight. Stores filled with young people, some of them—OK, most of them—not even born when I played here. It could work.

"You wouldn't mind?"

"Are you kidding? I'll text him right now. Plus, his dad, my brother? He's a huge Browns fan. All of us are, him and me and Ellen. Don't get to games that often, tickets are so darned expensive. But still love 'em."

"Even with their record?" Just a couple of seasons ago the Browns had gone 0 and 16. They were so bad Excedrin chipped in money for a parade celebrating their "perfect season."

Claire laughed. "They're like relatives. You should know that better than anybody. You don't have to like 'em—you just have to love 'em."

I nodded. I took her up on her offer. I didn't bother mentioning that people in Columbus saw it differently when it came to athletes who botched dreams of athletic glory.

Details with her nephew worked out, I paid my bill and left the restaurant, keeping an eye out for Bay Front's finest. Twenty minutes later I was shaking hands with her nephew, a lanky, affable kid who set me up in a corner with a MacBook with internet access. I opened a browser and searched for the Cuyahoga County auditor's website. I pulled up Schiff's Lake Avenue property again and this time spent several minutes studying the information in front of me. If I was breaching the walls of his castle, I wanted to know as much as possible about the inner layout. I had time to kill—I might as well make the most of it. I might not get another chance.

51

I WAS THINKING ABOUT the Lake Erie beach and gulls and Cheetos when Bonnie called.

"How are you feeling?"

"Pretty good," she said. "I just woke up from a two-hour nap. I could get used to this."

"Sleep now while you can. What's up?"

"I did some more poking around and found out something else. About PG Inc."

"Like what?"

"Well, we know they're a company that builds these server farms for the big guys, like Facebook and Google. And Amazon."

"I remember. And Flota."

"That's right. And you remember the project I told you about in Indiana?"

I told her I did.

"I found out why it never got off the ground. It's in an Indiana EPA filing that's kind of buried. Before the project went fully public, they did an environmental assessment, and it turns out there's a kind of crane that summers nearby. PG Inc. couldn't get the plans through."

"A crane?"

"That's right. And it must have been a rock-solid assessment, otherwise they would have just paved over those birds. Reminds me of that thing with Ed Sheeran and the skylark."

"Who's Ed Sheeran?"

She paused. "Only, like, the most famous singer on the planet right now?"

"Did he record in the 1980s?"

"Record? I don't think he was even born then."

"His loss. So what about him?"

"Couple years ago they had to move a concert he was doing in Germany because of concerns about the environmental impact on skylarks. That's a kind of bird—"

"I know what skylarks are," I said, thinking of my dad. "What it reminds *me* of is the coastal tanager situation. Anything else in that filing?"

"Maybe. A little something more about PG Inc."

"What about it?"

"How it got its name. The Indiana project? It was code-named Project Galleon."

"What?"

She repeated the name.

Project Galleon. PG Inc. I said, "Back to this crane. You think—?"

"I don't know what to think. I'm just telling you what I found. Maybe the company settled on a new site, at that swamp in Columbus, and wised up on dealing with environmental stuff."

It was yet another complicated piece of an already complicated puzzle. But it also helped put the stakes involving two swamps in Ohio in context. A massive computing facility made sense in Columbus, a city banking its future on high-tech jobs. Mostly left out of the industrial age that built robber baron metropolises like Cincinnati and Cleveland, the city was now fully embracing the digital age and the jobs it would bring. A couple years back it even made the top-twenty list for Amazon's new headquarters. The city was on the brink—

I stopped myself midthought and pictured myself in Schiff's office earlier in the day. His sermon on technology and the future. The origins of Flota—the silver fleet of the conquistadores. *They couldn't build ships fast enough.*

What if Bonnie's surmise was correct? What if PG Inc., through the efforts of Schiff, had given up on the Indiana location of a massive AI processing facility, but not the concept? What if they found a new home for it, with the only thing in the way a measly patch of wetlands and a nearly moribund bird species? What if they learned a lesson from those pesky cranes? And if so, what better place for the new, improved project than Columbus, named for the man whose voyages paved the way for the development of the Spanish sailing ships that transported riches during the Age of Discovery?

What better place for Flota and a project code-named Galleon?

52

I ENCOURAGED BONNIE TO keep her fluids up and told her I'd be back in touch. Checking the time, I sought out Claire's nephew, thanked him for all he'd done, and agreed to give him a selfie for his dad. I asked him not to post it on social media for a day. He looked at me puzzled, as if I'd asked him to forgo breathing, but after a couple moments he nodded. I left the store, parked myself in the food court, and ate two slices of pizza. Just as I finished, I received a call from Kym about Mike's upcoming scrimmage. I assured her again that I would be there. She asked if I was *sure* sure. I said that I was.

I was headed for my van, shadows lengthening as night approached, when Gloria called. It was 8:11 p.m.

"We're ten minutes off."

"Are you OK?"

"I'm still wrapping my mind around Big Dog."

"What do you mean?"

"Have you met him? He's like a mountain crossed with a tattoo parlor. I think he's the biggest guy I've ever seen."

"Sorry, should have warned you. Should I lie and tell you he's just a big teddy bear on the inside?"

"It's OK. We don't need teddy bears tonight."

"Which is the reason Otto uses him." Then I said, "Hey Gloria."

"What?"

"You're sure you're OK doing this? It's not your fight."

"Yes, I'm sure. And hell yes, it's my fight. I already gave you my spiel about this being my home. I was born and raised here, and I'm not going anyplace. Ten years in the military didn't change that. I'm tired of whoever's yanking my chain keeping me from doing my job and maybe screwing up my grandkids' future. And I need to find out once and for all what happened to Todd."

"Be careful, all right?"

"Don't go all lovey-dovey on me, Hayes. That was then, this is now. We've got more important things to think about."

"That was twelve hours ago."

"Time flies, even in the sticks. I'll call as soon as we know something."

I thanked her, started the van, and headed north, back to Lake Avenue. A few minutes later I was once again passing Schiff's house. The gate was rolled firmly shut. Lights on inside, buttery yellow at this distance, but no figures visible. For a moment I thought about parking by the fence and rushing the front of the house, stealth and subterfuge be damned. What did I have to lose at this point? But then I thought of Gloria and Otto and the risk they were taking. If there were cameras trained on the driveway, barreling in like a fool, heroic or not, wouldn't do much good if Schiff or somebody shot me down before I made it to the welcome mat. Instead, I continued back to the city park just down the road. I parked on the far end of the lot, which was clear of cops for now. I glanced at the Louisville Slugger. I picked it up and rubbed my hand over the smooth, polished ash. I set it down again. I'd need both hands for what I was doing tonight.

I descended the stairs and set off down the beach. I hugged the cliff rising to the houses above whenever possible, hoping to hide my progress from residents taking in an evening view of the lake. It would have been hard to blame them. A nearly full moon illuminated ridges of cirrus clouds stretching to the horizon. Down below the moonlight reflected off similar ridges of rippling water in the lake surface. Swallows swooped back and forth in balletic arcs as they nabbed mosquitoes. A perfect night for a stroll.

Three minutes later, setting my right foot on the bottom step of the rickety staircase leading up the cliff to Schiff's house, I questioned the wisdom of this approach. The weathered wooden structure shifted and creaked at the weight of my first foot plant. But what choice did I have? It was too late to run back to my van, drive to the front entrance, and tackle the assault that way. Ditto for me lumbering farther down the beach to find a more secure approach. Gloria and company were rolling. It was now or never. Taking a breath, I put my left foot on the next tread up. I stopped, feeling my phone buzz in my pocket. I stepped down and retrieved it. I had a text from Pete Henderson, at the U.S. Attorney's Office. I stared at the message.

My God, I thought, reading it.

How could I have been so stupid?

I replied, tucked the phone in my rear pocket, and glanced around. My eyes settled for a moment on the boulders lining the ground beneath Schiff's deck. Edges like the razor back of a slain dragon. I turned my gaze upward, stepped back onto the rickety staircase, and started climbing.

53

A THIRD OF THE way up I encountered my first spiderweb, draped across the staircase at forehead height. I felt a primordial chill in my stomach as I stopped and wiped the thick strands off my face while praying its resident was elsewhere for the evening. I took another step up.

Crack.

I froze. I looked down. Even in the fading light I saw that a line the length and width of a vein had opened up in the tread. I gripped the railings, sweat beading on my face, forearms bulging with tension, and carefully lifted my right foot onto the next step. Satisfied it would hold, I brought my left foot up. I waited. Nothing. I stepped up to the next tread, and the one after that. So far so good. I continued climbing.

Two-thirds of the way up I stopped again as the staircase swayed and I heard more cracks. I held still. I glanced to the right and caught a glimpse of small, gleaming eyes in the cliff wall that disappeared a second later. Mouse? I snuck a peek at the rocks on the beach below. Dragon? I breathed in and out, trying to relax. I thought again about turning around, before recalling Gloria's speech about reclaiming her home. I envied her. Being honest about it, I'd never felt as completely at peace in Columbus—or Cleveland, or anywhere—as growing up in Homer. And probably never would. I might never reclaim my roots. But maybe I could help Gloria protect hers from the corruption that had invaded her world. Shaking the thoughts away, I continued climbing.

A minute later I reached the top. I peered over the edge of the deck and looked onto the same patio where I'd seen Schiff that afternoon gazing at the lake like a sea captain contemplating a return voyage from the New World, hold groaning with gold. Before me a wall of glass ran the width of the house, inside of which I could make out the chairs and table of the main dining room. Unoccupied, as far as I could see. Lights on in the living room beyond that. Movement deeper inside.

I glanced up. Exterior lights positioned on either corner of the roof, but no cameras. I stepped onto the deck. Crouching like a man with a crick in his back, I scurried right, toward a sliding glass door. I crept up and tried it. Unlocked. I had no time to decide if this was a good or bad thing, or meant anything at all. I reached into my pocket, pulled out my phone, and looked for any word from Gloria or Otto. The faces of me and my boys stared back at me, but the screen was otherwise blank. I replaced the phone, reached over, and grabbed the patio door handle. I held my breath at the sound of the glass door rumbling over the runner like distant August thunder, and stepped inside.

"Hello, Andy," a man's voice said. "I would hold it right there if I were you."

54

I WAS STANDING IN an empty dining room, the gleaming oak table bare except for a single wine glass. The air was cool and smelled of cedar, something grilled, and recently snuffed candles. To my right was the entrance to the kitchen. Tiny green and red and white lights—power buttons, charging cords, digital clocks—blinked in the dark, their glow speaking to the ubiquitous presence of electronic utensils in our lives. Was pure darkness even possible anymore? I thought of Flota and the computing power it would provide, the legion of glowing lights on untold devices it would enable in the future. All those talking toasters. *They couldn't build ships fast enough.* Ahead of me, up a set of flagstone steps, the living room. I dropped my hands, opened them to show I wasn't armed, turned them palm forward, and took a step up, then another.

"That's close enough."

To my left, standing before a fireplace big enough to roast one of my uncle's pigs, and not a small one, stood Schiff. His right hand rested casually atop a lethal-looking iron poker. An easy match for my Louisville Slugger, if I'd gone that route. It was Schiff who had spoken. He'd changed clothes since our encounter in his office and was now dressed casually, in tan slacks, deck shoes, and an open-collar golf shirt. He looked like a man bound for a moonlight yacht ride. Next to him, on the edge of the L of a sectional leather couch, sat Laura. Her face was pale and wan, her expression that of a person recuperating from a long bout of influenza. Expecting to see relief in her eyes at my presence, I saw resignation instead. She stared at me, but I wasn't sure she was seeing anything. Standing beside her was Not Gary Phipps of Springfield, Missouri. Tear Drop to you and me. No knife for him tonight, I realized, eyeing the gun in his hand. I wondered idly if I'd ever know his real name.

"You certainly know how to make an entrance," Schiff said. "Now, if you would—"

I cut him off. "It's over. Let Laura come with me. I'm not interested in you or *you*." I nodded at Tear Drop. "Head out and kill as many endangered birds as you want. Go crazy and fricassee 'em if you want. Just let her go."

"Andy . . ." Laura said, her voice as low and weak as her face was fatigued.

"Laura and I were just finishing up a discussion," Schiff said. "After that, it's up to her what she wants to do."

"Has she been locked up here the whole time? If you did anything—"

"She's fine, as you can see. Not that you're really in a position to carry out any threats."

"Andy . . ."

"Are you all right?" I directed the question to the judge.

"I said she's fine," Schiff interrupted. "But I'm going to have to ask you to go with Eric here." He nodded at Tear Drop.

"Go where? The bottom of a swamp?"

"Just downstairs."

"To where you've got Todd Orick? Or what's left of him?"

Laura flinched at the name.

"Andy. They have Daniel."

"Daniel?" I said carefully.

"My *son*. They've got him. And they're going to—"

"We're not going to do anything," Schiff said, frustration in his voice. "This is the point I've been trying to make, Laura.

226

Nothing's happening as long as we come to a simple agreement. One mutually beneficial to us all, I might add."

She shook her head helplessly. I looked at the widescreen TV on the wall opposite the fireplace, and the control box below. A blue light indicated the time was 8:22. What was happening in Mohican Township?

"Agreement?" I said to Schiff. "Is that the new legal term for extortion? Or is it blackmail?"

"Extortion?" Schiff said.

"The Berman Prize?"

"So we're back to that, are we?"

I willed my phone to buzz with news from Otto. But it stayed silent in my pocket. I traded glances with Eric aka Gary Phipps aka Tear Drop. There was a familiar gleam in his eyes I couldn't place at first. Then I remembered where I'd seen it last: in the frozen eyes of all those dead coastal tanagers.

"You knew Laura used a forged recommendation from Judge Northcott to secure that internship, didn't you?"

Schiff didn't react. But for the first time since stepping inside I had Laura's full attention.

"You knew her secret."

"Secret?"

"That her success was based on a lie."

The judge stirred. "Andy . . . "

"There were just a couple things I couldn't figure out. Laura—an academic swindler? It didn't make sense, what I knew of her. But even if that was possible, how did you know? It's obvious now you confronted her with it—perfect leverage for forcing a Mendon Woods ruling in your favor. But who tipped you off? And how or why, so many years later?"

"Eric," Schiff said, voice as cold as the bottom of a freezer. "Take him downstairs. The room on the right."

I took a step back, closer to the dining room and the patio door I'd entered through. The door was still open, letting in a cooling night breeze.

"But I had it all wrong, didn't I?" I said to Schiff. "You didn't come across the information. You knew about the forged letter from the beginning. All the way back to your days as Laura's study buddy."

"Eric."

"You knew, because you wrote it."

"*Eric.*"

I took another step back. Thought of the text I'd gotten from Pete Henderson just as I started my ascent.

Not sure why you had me check something you already seemed to know. But you're right. Randall Schiff interned with Judge Northcott one summer in law school. Also, you can go to hell.

I looked at Schiff. I said, "Raabe, Karabinus, Northcott, Rickard and Dowd."

Schiff was quiet. Laura stared at him, eyes bright.

"Let me guess," I said. "Laura's in a panic about the Berman Prize and the public-service component. You're still secretly angry about the breakup. You see an opportunity. You're interning for Judge Northcott—your families were neighbors, so making the connection was easy, right? Once you were there, how hard could it have been to lift some stationery? I can only imagine Laura's surprise"—I stared at her, locking our gaze—"her *relief* when you presented her with the letter she needed to finish her application to the DOJ. The one thing she hadn't been able to secure. She gets what she needs. And so do you."

Schiff looked at me impatiently. "I do?"

"You have a secret. Something to hold over Laura should you ever need it."

Schiff shook his head and nodded at Tear Drop.

"Let's go," Eric said, raising the gun. "Enough with the fucking monologue already."

55

I KEPT MY EYES on Laura. I had to see what she was thinking. What was going through her mind.

"What was the deal?" I said. "She rules against the coastal tanager and you go away with her secret safe? But she resisted, didn't she, even when you confronted her with something that could destroy her career? Because she's the Velvet Fist"—I emphasized the phrase, never looking away from Laura—"and doesn't give up easily. You had to raise the stakes. Up the ante. Bring her family into it."

Laura's eyes widened.

"You had to threaten her son. Of all the cheap, tawdry tricks. A dead bird in his apartment. *Godfather* lite. Yeah, that got her attention. But you weren't counting on her coming after you, were you? Coming up here in person? So then you had to ratchet things up even more." I paused. "You had to take her son. Just like you took Todd Orick."

An inhalation from Schiff. A flicker in Laura's eyes. Still shiny, but no longer with resignation.

Now came the biggest gamble of all. Keeping my eyes locked on Laura's, I said, "I'm sorry. I know what they did to Daniel. And I'm afraid I have to tell you something. Something that's not good."

"What?" Laura said, panic filling her eyes.

"I'm so sorry."

"Tell me what?"

I glanced at Schiff and shook my head.

Laura's eyes burned bright with rage.

"That's not true," Schiff said, glancing at Tear Drop. "We didn't do—"

"How could you?" I said. "He was the world to Laura. Her only son—"

"That's not true—"

He never got the chance to finish. In an instant Laura was off the couch and clawing at Schiff, hands scrabbling for his throat, an inarticulate sound coming from her, frightening to hear from someone who always knew the right words to say. Startled, trying to defend himself, Schiff let go the poker, stepped back, lost his balance, and tumbled over. I didn't hesitate. I threw myself at Eric aka Tear Drop, his attention momentarily drawn to the melee beside the fireplace. He and I went flying over the edge of the couch at the impact of my charge. I wrestled his gun hand up over his head. We rolled across the cool, paved stone floor, each grappling for purchase. I heard explosions—one, two, three—as he fired the gun involuntarily. Glass shattered, the dining-room viewing window collapsed, and a wave of cool air like a storm front rushed into the house. I reached and grabbed the gun. With his left hand Eric gouged my eyes. I squeezed them tight, trying to avoid his sharp fingernails. I loosened the gun from his grip and tossed it away from me, toward the patio.

A mistake. At the sound of the gun landing behind us, Eric let go my face and rolled free of my grip like a wrestler escaping the ring. He stood up and darted toward the weapon, shoes crunching on broken glass littering the floor. I rose with a grunt and chased.

He made it almost to a first down before I tackled him as he bent low to retrieve the gun. We went down and rolled around again. Over once. Over twice. Three times but still no jackpot.

Now outside, on the deck. Finally, back on top, trying to pin him beneath me. I thought it was over when he jerked his right knee upward between my legs and I saw more stars than properly belonged in the night sky over Cleveland. My stomach flip-flopped with nausea and I released my grip. He scooted back. Hearing more than seeing, I thrust out my hands and grabbed his legs and tried to pull him close. He sat up, grabbed my left shoulder, and bit me. I shouted in pain and released him.

He stood, staggered a bit as he regained his balance, looked down, and bent to retrieve the gun. I pushed myself up on my knees and half-crawled, half-crab-walked into his reclined body. I pushed him forward, toward the edge of the deck. He kicked me and my head snapped back and I saw stars again, this time from beyond the Milky Way. I cleared my vision, looked up, and saw him with the gun in his hand, backing up, readying his aim.

"Wait—" I said.

Too late. He realized at the last moment he'd misjudged his steps. He was too far back, stumbling as he stepped onto the first of the rickety stairs leading to the beach. There was a loud crack and he dropped a foot, then two, as the structure buckled. He swung his arms, cartwheeling, trying to gain his balance. At the last moment he reached and grabbed one edge of the railing with his free hand.

"Drop the gun!" I yelled.

He swore at me, something like a half-grin on his face, and shook his head. I backed up, hearing another crack. His eyes got big and he swung his arm crazily in the air, like a man at a track urging on runners in a race. Then he lost his grip and disappeared as the stairs fell away altogether. A final scream drowned out by the sound of crashing wood. Even so, it was easy to hear the impact of his body striking the boulders below. Lake Erie has never been big on sandy beaches.

I STOOD, CATCHING MY breath. But only for a second. I heard Laura cry out inside the house. I stumbled as I ran, nearly slipping and falling on the shards of glass littering the dining room's smooth stone floor.

She stood beside the fireplace over Schiff, who lay curled in a fetal position, his face bloodied. In her hand she held the fireplace poker. The Velvet Fist, indeed. She raised it—

"Laura, no!"

She glanced at me wildly.

"He killed Daniel! He killed my son—"

"No!"

"You said!"

I stepped back. I pulled out my phone. It was buzzing with a call.

"Wait," I said to the judge. "Just wait."

"Woody."

Otto.

"Did you—"

"We got him. We got the kid. But listen, it didn't go down exactly right."

"What happened?"

"Gloria," he said. "That cop. She—"

"She what?"

Nothing.

"Otto!"

But the line had gone dead.

56

I PUNCHED REDIAL. THE phone rang but no one picked up. I tried again in vain. I turned back to the judge. She stood there, poker in hand, staring at me. Schiff tried to inch backwards. She raised the poker and he froze.

"Daniel—" she said.

"No," I said. "He's alive. They got him."

"Who? Who got him? You said—"

Gloria. That cop. She—

She what?

"I know what I said. It wasn't true. I was bluffing. Daniel's OK."

"How do you know?" she demanded.

"They rescued him. It's going to be—"

"*Who* rescued him?"

"Friends of mine."

"Who? How? Let me talk to him."

"I can't—"

"Why not?"

"The phone—"

But even as I spoke the phone buzzed again. This time the ring tone of a FaceTime call. The ID said Otto. With a trembling finger I pressed the green disk to accept the call.

"Otto. What's going—"

"Hayes."

Gloria stared at me from the screen. She brushed wisps of hair out of her eyes.

"Gloria, are you all right? Otto said—"

"I'm fine. I'm just not going to be sitting around on my ass for a while. Bastard nailed me in the right cheek. Never should have let him get the drop on me like that." She shook her head.

"Thank God. But what about—"

Gloria's face swam away. For a moment the screen was black, then it filled with blurred shadows. Green blades of corn leaves flicked past in the background. A moment later a young man's face appeared. Dark hair, eyes set deep in sockets. Prominent, patrician brow. He stared at me, confused. I stepped forward, and handed the phone to Laura. She took it, hand shaking, and gasped.

"Daniel?"

"Mom?"

I TOOK THE PHONE back two minutes later. Now Laura's eyes were shiny with something besides rage. But she maintained her vigilance over Schiff, threatening him with the poker each time he groaned and asked for mercy. He was bleeding from a gash on the forehead where the judge's first two blows struck. But he remained conscious, watching Laura with fear in his Caribbean-blue eyes.

"Woody."

Otto, back on FaceTime. In comparison to the pain on Gloria's face, he looked exhilarated.

"We're good. Help's on the way."

I panicked. "No. The county people. You can't trust them. I told you—"

"Relax. I called a buddy of mine with the state patrol. They got a whole phalanx coming."

"A phalanx?"

"Like Greek warriors. Read some history for a change, Woody. Anyway, them at least we can trust."

We talked for another minute. I explained what happened in Bay Front. I had just asked him to pass the phone back to Gloria when a sound interrupted me. A pounding at the front door. I moved to answer it, but never got a chance. A moment later it burst open and three men in the uniforms of the Bay Front Police Department rushed inside.

"Freeze!"

"Ta-ta for now," I said to Otto, dropping the phone as I raised my hands.

57

"IT'S MY BIRTHDAY TODAY, you know. I was going to take the day off. Try to make up for the time I lost screwing around with you."

"Many happy returns," I said, staring up at Franklin County sheriff's detective Chad Pinney. It was a difficult maneuver, with my hands shackled to a table in a holding room of the Bay Front City Jail, the walls the color of used Juicy Fruit. My belongings, including my wallet and phone and my favorite Timex sports watch, were long gone. I estimated it was between one and two o'clock in the morning the following day. He'd made good time from Columbus.

"Do you know how much trouble you're in?"

"I could hazard a guess. But I bet it's not as much as some folks in Mohican Township. And you may not smell so sweet yourself, given that I tried to explain all this three days ago and you told me to go pound salt."

"Listen—"

"Listen yourself. For one thing—"

Fortunately for my rap sheet, a Bay Front jail guard interrupted my soliloquy with the news that a lawyer was in the lobby instructing Pinney and the two Bay Front detectives lined up behind him to desist from any questioning of his client, namely me.

Thank goodness Burke Cunningham is a night owl.

And a tough one at that.

TEAR DROP WAS DEAD. Gary Phipps of Springfield, Missouri, turned out to be Eric Weiler, a dirty-tricks man Schiff employed over the years after first encountering him at his apartment complex. Where a fellow resident complained he'd seen Weiler breaking into cars in the parking lot with a crude jimmy. Rather than evict him, Schiff hired Weiler and a few of his cronies as off-the-books employees. It took rescuers several minutes to reach the beach and the boulders, and by then he was long past help.

Schiff was in the hospital having his head stitched up and quite likely talking to his own lawyers. The fact he belonged in jail and not me wasn't lost on Cunningham, though he failed to persuade the Bay Front detectives or the city attorney in that argument. It might have been the time of day, which was in fact the middle of the night. Lots of people had been sound asleep when phones started ringing. A bedroom community, after all.

The judge was gone. We were separated as soon as the officers rushed in and saw the shattered window and the blood on Schiff's face. Cunningham did his best to find out how Laura was, and where, but he might as well have been asking Alexa to give an honest opinion of Siri.

FOR BREAKFAST, I ATE runny eggs and oatmeal a packet of sugar away from kindergarten paste. My dining companion was a guy about my age picked up during a traffic stop on an outstanding warrant for failure to pay child support.

"You're Woody Hayes," he said, bleary-eyed, as he moved his eggs from one side of a paper plate to another. "I saw your last game with the Clowns. Four interceptions—what the hell? What are you doing here?"

"Get it right—five interceptions. Franchise record. Though at least we won a few. You guys should try it some time. I'm here because I don't have any place better to be."

"That figures. Tell you what—biggest waste of money I ever heard of."

"What?"

"My season tickets. Hope springs eternal, I guess. Half the time I don't even bother going."

"You have season tickets to the worst team in the NFL and you're behind on child-support payments?"

"Allegedly behind, wise guy. What's it to you, anyway? We're wearing the same rags in the same lockup, in case you haven't noticed. You can stick the civics lessons up your ass."

I was about to inform him he had the same right when he interrupted me. "Much as it pains me to say this, you still got fans up here."

I thought of Claire in the Bay Diner. "One or two, maybe."

"More than that. My ex just put a signed jersey of yours on eBay. Belonged to me. Pissed me off, I'll tell you that, but she got $150 for it, so I guess I can't blame her."

"A hundred and fifty dollars?"

"What I said."

I thought for a second. "How 'bout I replace it?"

"What?"

"The jersey. Signed and everything. I'll give you two, in fact."

He looked at me suspiciously. "In exchange for what?"

I told him. He thought about it, and agreed. We closed the deal on a handshake.

So Claire and Ellen and their husbands would get to see a game this season after all. Somebody had to use those season tickets.

I spent most of the rest of the day reading a Les Roberts paperback from the jail library and trying to persuade the guards to get a message to the two Kevins regarding Hopalong and the judge's cat. It wasn't until a brief late-afternoon visit from Cunningham that I learned that Gloria was going to be all right, thanks to the ministrations of Otto as they waited for the ambulance and the troopers to arrive. She just wasn't going to be sitting down reading to a grandkid on her lap anytime soon.

I almost found myself missing the comforts of the Bay Front jail the next day, most of which I spent in a conference room in the Justice Center in downtown Cleveland, a fish-stick-colored gulag whose minimalist architecture was to traditional courthouses as poured concrete is to stained glass. In attendance were the county prosecutor, two assistant U.S. attorneys—one of them Pete Henderson, up from Columbus—a state patrol lieutenant, an FBI agent, a state Bureau of Criminal Investigation detective, Franklin County sheriff's detective Chad Pinney, Burke Cunningham, and yours truly. I spent more time than I could ever have imagined briefing the state's top law-enforcement officials about the migratory habits of the coastal tanager. I was working my way toward the topography of northeastern Brazil when a second FBI agent, a young African American woman, entered the room and whispered to her colleague and Henderson. A minute later Cunningham and I found ourselves summarily dismissed and sitting in chairs in a small lobby flipping through a day-old *Plain Dealer*.

"Any guesses?"

"Not really," Cunningham said. "It's probably not good."

It wasn't good.

After interviewing Gloria about the Todd Orick case, state crime-scene investigators blanketed Heyder's Creek. Fifteen people doing a search that Gloria often found herself doing alone. It didn't take long. They found what was left of the young man with the mischievous smile under a submerged log. We sat in silence as we took that news in. A few minutes later it was trumped by a new development in the form of an Associated Press news alert that popped up on Cunningham's phone. The Mohican County sheriff had been arrested on obstruction of justice charges.

58

JUST BEFORE NOON THE next day I knocked on the door at Gloria's house. A young woman who could have been her much younger sister opened the door, a toddler boy in her arms and a girl of about three clinging to her leg. The little girl held a stuffed horse. Taking me in, the look on the woman's face was as if Jeffrey Dahmer had come to call. She raised the ante to Ariel Castro when I gave her my name and explained why I was there.

"It's all right, Angie," Gloria called out. "He's a friend of mine." A pause followed by a weak laugh. "Even though he got me into this mess."

I stepped inside, offering a smile to Angie, which wasn't returned. Gloria was camped out on the couch, lying on her good side. Carl and Madeleine lay beneath her on the floor butt to butt, vigilance in their dark eyes as they examined the intruder. They also didn't return my smile.

I set a Styrofoam container on the coffee table. In it were roasted turkey slices slathered in gravy over white bread with mashed potatoes and peas from Down Home Buffet. Compliments of Bev. I accepted Gloria's invitation to sit in a chair. I asked her how she was feeling. She winced as she spoke. She wasn't expected back on duty for several weeks, which was probably all right, since there wasn't much left of the Mohican Township Police Department at this point anyway.

"That's the end of the wind turbine, that's for sure," she said, using her fork to cut the turkey into manageable bites. My offer to help won me an Angie-like glare I guessed was half cop, half pissed-off grandma, and I quickly backed off.

"Well, you said it wasn't all that popular."

"It wasn't. And the dead birds didn't help."

"Even though that was faked."

"I'm hearing now that was part of the deal," she said.

"What do you mean?"

"Schiff and them cooked it up. County keeps its hands off anything happening at Heyder's Creek. In exchange, birds keep getting dumped at the base of the turbine, which nobody wants anyway and which sure as hell won't be joined by others. Win-win. Well, except for the birds."

"I wonder if it's too late for them."

"Don't know," Gloria said. "But there's already talk the state may move in and take control of Heyder's Creek. Turn it into a sanctuary. Try to restore the birds. You think that's possible?"

"Maybe. Mendon Woods is not going anywhere anytime soon, that's for sure. Not after all this." The news had been full of the events of the last few days. The Natural Resources Department had already filed a motion for summary judgment in its favor. The case had been given to a new judge, but the outcome seemed good for the swamp either way. For PG Inc. and Flota and a billion-dollar artificial intelligence server farm, not so much.

"I won't keep you any longer. I'm just glad to see you're—"

Angie stared at me from across the room.

"Glad you're going to be all right."

"No thanks to you, Hayes," Gloria said with a wink.

OLD LABRADOR OR NOT, Hopalong mustered something resembling actual enthusiasm when I opened my front door just over an hour later, if you count a muzzle thrust into my crotch along with a vigorous tail-wagging as a sign of affection. I tried not to tear up, the bruises from Tear Drop's knee to the groin still fresh. The reception from Laura's cat was more muted, consisting as it did of its—I still wasn't sure its gender—contemplating me from a perch on the back of the couch as it blinked its yellow eyes with equal parts skepticism and ennui. Seeing the cat underscored the importance of the call I needed to make. But as I had all day up to this point, I put it off. Instead, I rang up Theresa to thank her for her help.

"Not a problem, QB. We were just talking about how cool it was it turned out this way."

"We?"

"Ben and me."

"Who's Ben?"

"The guy from the gym. Wanted to be my personal trainer. Remember, I stuck my—"

"Yes, I remember. You talked to him?"

"We had a date. Last night."

I processed the information. "You went on a date with the guy you met at the gym where the judge's son worked?"

"Don't sound so surprised, QB. We had a good time. He behaved himself."

"What did you do?"

"I made him hand out soap. Then we went for ice cream at UDF."

I tried to picture Theresa and a guy from a gym handing out toiletries to trafficked women on the city's west side and then taking in fine dining at United Dairy Farmer. I supposed as a first date it was as good as any.

"How's that judge doing?" Theresa said.

"I'm not sure. OK, I think."

"You're not sure? Haven't you talked to her?"

"Not since—well, not since everything happened."

"You save your girlfriend and her son and you ain't talked to her yet?"

"She's not my girlfriend." I recalled my similar protestations to Gloria.

"Really? What is she, QB?"

A damned good question. And one I knew I needed an answer to sooner rather than later.

59

AFTER HANGING UP, I opened a can of Black Label, took it down to half-mast, walked around the apartment, picked up the cat, determined at last through close inspection—investigator, remember?—that it was male, set him down, went back into the kitchen, finished the beer, and called Laura. She didn't pick up. I left her a short voice mail. On further consideration, I also texted her a picture of the cat. Just in case you were worried.

No response. Then, a minute later: Don't give him wet food. And that was it. No other message.

I tried the following day, but she didn't answer, call or text. I wasn't sure I blamed her. The headlines had been unrelenting. Some were sympathetic to Laura, but a fair share questioned whether she could have done more and should or could have told the authorities what was happening earlier. An equal split on whether she'd known the truth about the judge's recommendation for the Berman Prize all along. Either way, after a weekend of radio silence, I figured, right or wrong, that Laura was done with me, and who could blame her. And that now I was a cat owner. Oh joy.

Tuesday morning, I sat on the couch with my laptop and watched online as Laura held a news conference in her chambers. It was quite a performance. Alone in her chair, she answered questions for forty-five minutes. Nothing was off-limits. She answered forthrightly, coming off as neither blameless nor beaten. I wasn't sure it would save her Supreme Court campaign, let alone her judicial career, but you could tell by the end that the room of reporters was on her side.

She did good.

Bonnie, texting me.

You watched?

In between looking up stuff on cribs. You think you might have time to talk to Troy this week?

Sure, I responded. We'll grab that beer and a burger.

He's vegan lol

I'm allergic to tofu.

Don't be a baby. North Star has good veggie burgers AND beer

In that case it's a date.

I logged off, threw on my running clothes, and headed to Schiller Park. I did four loops around, picking up the pace on the last lap to just faster than a quick jaywalk. I jogged back to the bottom of Mohawk and walked the rest of the way to my house. I came inside, stretched, and did twenty pull-ups on the bar stretched across the kitchen entrance way. I got down on the floor and did forty sit-ups. I rested, and prepared to try forty more. I heard my ringtone go off. I looked at the number.

Laura calling.

"Hello?"

"It's me. I'm sorry I haven't been available. I was wondering if you were free."

I said, "There's no need to apologize. I'm just glad to hear from you. I watched you, talking to the reporters. Good job."

"Thank you."

"Are you all right?"

"I don't know. I'm still trying to sort everything out, to be honest."

"That makes two of us. How's Daniel?"

She told me he was having a rough time of it, but she thought he'd be all right eventually.

I said, "I can sneak up to your condo, if you'd like. Park across the street so—"

"Are you home?"

"Home?"

"Yes. The place you live?"

I told her I was.

"Would it be all right if I stopped by?"

"Of course. But aren't you afraid of people—"

"I'll see you soon."

I jumped in the shower. She arrived twenty minutes later. I invited her in, kissed her on the cheek, and showed her into the living room.

"*Oliver*," she said, walking to the couch, picking up the cat and pressing him to her chest.

She said, "I thought he was lost, before your text. I thought they'd . . . All this time?"

"I brought him here that first morning. I didn't want him there alone. I didn't know, you know, how long you might be gone. Some friends looked after him and the dog when I was away."

"Thank you, Andy." She settled herself on the couch, Oliver secure in her arms. I went into the kitchen and poured us both glasses of water. I set hers on the coffee table in front of the couch and sat in the chair opposite her.

I said, "It's good to see you. I'm glad you're all right."

"I'm alive, anyway. Thanks to you."

"Maybe. But I'm not the one who clocked Schiff in the snout."

"Don't be a fool." She paused. "I'm sorry, that came out wrong. I reacted in the moment, hitting him like that. But if you hadn't shown up . . . "

I nodded, not permitting myself to speak, and took a sip of water.

"So again, thanks."

"You're welcome. So, what's next for you?"

"I'm not really sure."

"What do you mean?"

"Well, you've seen the articles and editorials, no doubt. I thought the news conference went well, but that's just public opinion, in the end. There are rules of judicial conduct and legal ethics to contend with. Plus, right before the reporters arrived I got a call from the state party chairman. They want me to step down, let the governor appoint a replacement for the remainder of my term. And forget about the campaign. The bar association too. I heard from *them* yesterday."

"Step down why?"

"They think the experience has poisoned my impartiality. That it would make it impossible for me to oversee cases going forward."

"What do you think?"

"I think I'm not going to decide today. I have more important things to focus on."

"Like what?"

"Like what I just said—thanking you. For coming after me. For not giving up, even after I disappeared. You would have been within your rights to walk away, you know."

"I don't think so. But there's also the little matter of the call that night. That's what really caught my attention."

"The what?"

"The missed call, at midnight or whatever. That's why I went to your condo the next day. I took it as a cry for help. That you couldn't tell me something earlier that evening, but somehow you managed to—"

I stopped. Her face had gone as pale as the blank side of a legal brief.

"You got a call from me?"

"A missed call. That's right."

"Andy," she said softly. "I didn't call. I mean, not on purpose. This is the first I've heard of it. I still had my phone, at Schiff's house, until they remembered to take it from me. It must have been a misdial—"

"You're sure?"

She nodded, unable to speak.

"But the clues. 'Practically zero percent feelings.' *Estoppel.* The paper in the book by your bed. Weren't you—"

"Being a little melodramatic? I thought so at the time. Less so when the sheriff's detective called and told me you were in his office. But when I left for Cleveland, I never dreamed all that would be necessary. It was out of desperation, I guess, in case I . . . The point is, I didn't call on purpose. And then they took my phone, and my license. Thank God they let me answer when the detective called."

I thought about something. "The safe phrase."

"What?"

"Pinney said you have a safe phrase, in case you're ever in trouble. You didn't use it that day, which threw him off."

"That's right."

"What is it?"

"It's a little silly."

"Try me."

"It's 'vacuum fixed.'"

"What?"

"As in, 'I'm fine, just running some errands. And getting the vacuum fixed.' V.F. Like—"

"Like 'Velvet Fist.'"

She nodded, giving up a small smile.

Neither of us said anything for a moment. I pondered what might have happened if Laura's phone hadn't accidentally called me. If I hadn't made a split-second decision to drive to her condo and check up on her. If I hadn't returned to search her apartment more closely after Mike's off-handed comment as we tossed the pigskin back and forth. *1 percent . . .*

I rose from my chair and walked over to the couch. I sat and put my arm around her. She tensed at the touch, just for a moment, then rested her head on my shoulder. We sat that way for a minute, saying nothing, listening to ourselves breathe. Then she raised her head, reached a hand to my chin, and pulled me close.

"Oh, Andy," she said. She kissed me lightly on the lips. "If you—"

"I know. It's a scary thought. But sometimes the universe gets it right." I returned the kiss a little more forcefully. A moment later the cat found itself off Laura's lap and on the floor. It took a little longer today than the night in her car, but soon my hands were under her shirt and hers were on the buttons of my jeans.

"You still have closing arguments to wrap up," Laura said after another minute. "You didn't get a chance to finish the other night."

"That would be my assessment."

"In that case, please proceed. Expeditiously."

"Yes, your honor."

AFTERWARD, AS WE LAY beside each other on my bed, Laura reached over and took my hand. Surprised, I waited a moment before lacing my fingers with hers.

"I was thinking," Laura said.

"Oh?"

"You know where Bethel Road is?"

"Of course."

"You know how it's this mecca of Indian and Asian restaurants."

"Yes," I said, uncertainly.

"So there's a new Thai place up there. Just opened."

I didn't answer right away. I'd had this conversation before. With Laura, the last time we'd been together in bed. Some years ago now. The questions and answers reversed, but the content the same.

"Laura—"

"Got a good review in the paper. I was thinking of trying it out. Maybe for dinner. Or even lunch."

"Listen—"

"Thinking *we* should try it out."

I let go of her hand and shifted onto my side to face her.

"What are you saying?"

"I'm saying we should try a new Thai place. It's been suggested before, you may recall."

"I recall, believe me. My question is, what are you saying beyond that?"

"I understood the nature of your interrogatory the first time."

"Then answer the damn thing. If you please."

"The answer is, I don't know."

"OK . . ."

"I don't know what I'm asking you, beyond suggesting we go to lunch. I'm not suggesting more than that for the moment. I know I've missed your company—in and out of bed," she added quickly.

"And I've missed yours."

"I suspect you're lying, but that's all right. If you are, I deserve it. If you're not, I'm pleased. But either way, I don't know what I'm ready for. I'm still a person who craves her privacy, and who worries about commitment. None of that's changed. What has is the permission I'm giving myself to reexamine my arguments."

"In light of new evidence?"

"Something like that. So what do you think?"

I thought briefly of Gloria, and our night—and morning—together in her house. Of the contentment she expressed at her life when she made it clear, politely but firmly, she wouldn't be road-tripping to Columbus to see me anytime soon. I wondered what it would be like to be comfortable in your skin like that, to feel you belonged to a place that was home in the deepest way possible. I wondered if I'd ever see her again.

I said, "I've realized over the past few days how much I care for you. That's the truth. But I'm also a person who craves privacy, and worries about commitment."

"Except when it comes to rescuing damsels in distress."

"Perhaps. What I meant was, it's not like in my salad days, when I thought commitment was for suckers. These days it's an occupational hazard."

"What do you mean?"

"Who wants a boyfriend who's always getting shot at? Beat up? Or worst of all, always running late?"

I closed my eyes for a moment and thought of my ex-girlfriend Anne. Opened them a second later and took in the judge's face.

She said, "I see your point. Puts a damper on dinner and a movie."

"Not to mention arguments over whose turn it is to walk the dog."

"Back to us," she said. "I don't know what I'm ready for. It could be this"—she patted my thigh—"or it could be something more. But right now, either way, I'm hoping it involves some Thai food. Let's go."

"Now? In the middle of the day? Anyone could see us—"

"After what I've been through? Like I give a shit," the Velvet Fist said, rising from my bed and reaching for her clothes.

60

THE FOLLOWING FRIDAY NIGHT I sat high in crowded bleachers as Mike's opening high school scrimmage played out on the field before me. Blue against gold. No pads and two-hand touch only. A fundraiser put on by the boosters. The late-summer air was soft and smelled of freshly cut grass and cooking meat and muscle liniment. Joe, Mike's half brother, sat on my right, his nose buried in the new Philip Pullman novel. To my left sat Mike's mom, Kym, my ex-wife. Her husband, Steve, Mike's stepdad, sat two rows down, casting a glance back at us now and then. Laura had politely declined my invitation to join me, citing time she wanted to spend with Daniel and his sister before she went back to college. I suspected the judge would have declined either way, but I wasn't about to make an issue of it. Sharing bowls of warm pad Thai and cold bottles of Singha in a crowded restaurant at high noon was accomplishment enough for a week.

Mike entered the game in the second quarter. He promptly threw an interception, sparking a chorus of groans in the stands and the less than subtle shifting of dozens of eyes in my direction, like nighttime predators mustering the courage to approach the firelight. But on Blue's next possession he marched the team downfield in just seven plays, and scored the touchdown himself with a last-second run into the corner. Two possessions later, he connected on passes of twenty-five and thirty-seven yards respectively before handing the ball off to a running back for another touchdown. Curiosity replaced recrimination in the eyes still brave enough to look at me.

"Chip off the old block," Kym said. "That's what they're saying, you know." She gestured at the fans, including her husband, their eyes locked on Mike.

"Which shows how wrong they are."

"What do you mean?"

"By the time I was Mike's age I'd already won a state championship and was on my way to a second. I had college scholarship offers at sixteen. He's a backup quarterback with a wobble to his spiral."

"Oh, that's real nice—"

"On the other hand," I interrupted, "I had Ds in most of my classes, except English, because I liked to read, and math, because my teacher happened to be my mom and she would have killed me otherwise. Mike, by contrast, is a straight-A student, has a job, and is also a pretty mean piano player, whereas my musical abilities stop and start with inserting Bon Jovi CDs into my car stereo."

Kym shook her head. "Mike's cocky, just like you, and football doesn't help with that. And I worry about all the girls hanging off him. He doesn't discourage them, believe me. And what if he gets knocked around? All this stuff about concussions—"

"All this stuff about concussions is serious. We're going to have to keep a close eye on that. I'm going to keep a close eye," I added. "But for right now, we have to focus on who Mike is. Not who his dad is. There's plenty of other people happy to do that job. They don't need any help from us."

"You're almost making sense tonight, Andy. I'm not sure how to respond."

"Maybe do what I do. Or what I'm trying to do more of."

"Which is what?"

"Pay attention to the game. Your son just passed for another touchdown."

She looked out at the field, where blue-shirted boys were mobbing Mike at the thirty-yard line.

"Our son, you mean," she said, standing to return to sit beside Steve.

Acknowledgments

Thanks to Donte Goosby and Mitch Stacy for help with the football passages, to Fred Alverson for a history lesson on the U.S. Attorney's Office in Columbus, to beer consultant Steve Goble, to Bill Parker for his law enforcement advice, and as always to real-life private eye Marty Yant for sharing his expertise. Special thanks to Doug Berman for answering questions about law school culture and grading systems and for lending his name to a fictional scholarship prize. A tip of the hat to the staff of Ohio University Press for everything they do to make my books better. This novel is dedicated to Pete Henderson in celebration of fifty years of friendship that began in second grade in Lima, New York, a long time ago in a galaxy far, far away. Looking forward to fifty more!